M A Y H E M

DEREK E DYKES

Mayhem: *the intentional and wanton removal of a body part that would handicap a person's ability to defend himself in combat. Under the strict common law definition, this required damage to an eye or a limb, while cutting off an ear or a nose, was deemed not sufficiently disabling. Later, the meaning of the crime expanded to encompass any mutilation, disfigurement, or crippling act, done using any instrument. The noun "mayhem", and the verb "maim", came from Old French "mahaigne".*

Book One:
MADNESS

Book Two:
MAYHEM

Special Thanks to Rebecca, April, Angela, Nicole and Amanda
And to all the true friends and family
who helped me through the best and worst times of my life.

1
❧Procurement❧

"I'll bid four-hundred thousand," I responded, holding my hand up for the auctioneer to see.

"Four-hundred thousand for each, or for the pair?" Grummold asked, gesturing toward them. It had never crossed my mind that even scum like Grummold would consider breaking them apart, but all eyes were on me now, and I had no time to argue the point.

"For the set, of course; don't go there again." I answered, feeling a roomful of eyes staring intently at me. "This auction was advertised as being for the pair." We were down to two bidders; me and a man who called himself 'Strong-arm'. Whether it was supposed to be his name, or his title I am not sure, but at the moment I really didn't care. All I wanted to do was win this auction, grab what I had come for, and get out of the Miami Dark Zone as fast as possible.

Grummold responded slyly, his vaguely Indian accent making him sound like more of an indentured servant from film noir than an auctioneer. "Of course - the bidding is for the pair. Yes, yes... so we continue now." Grummold placed his hands on the center of the bidding device and nodded his head toward Strong-arm. We each placed our hands on the flat metal plates in front of us, as Grummold announced, "Round Seventeen - place your bets!" The room behind us was filled to standing room only. With the announcement, the crowd started placing their wagers on which of us would pull our hands out first. Whoever held out longest was allowed to place their next bid on the set for auction. If a bidder lost three rounds in a row - they were out. Two days of this had passed, clearing out over a hundred participants. Strong-arm and I were the only ones left now, and we were both down to two losses each. This round would decide who took them home.

A bell was rung to stop the wagers from being placed in the room, and Grummold announced the beginning of the final round. The electricity arched over the top of my hands, much more intense than the last two-dozen shocks I'd already taken today. I looked over to Strong-arm to see him clenching his teeth so hard that a trickle of blood started to slowly crawl down his chin. As the seconds stretched on, the smell of ozone and searing flesh began to make me nauseous, but I dared not look to see if it was my own hands cooking, or if I was finally getting the best of Strong-arm. The roar of the crowd behind me began to fade off into the distance, replaced by the sensation of millions of biting ants on my arms, breasts and neck. When the voltage increased, I knew that if I blacked out, I would lose my chance. I looked to the small stage behind Grummold, seeing them huddled together, imagining them to be horrified at the spectacle of violence before them. "I'm no good to you dead," I thought to myself, and prepared to raise my hands from the metal plates.

My opponent apparently had other plans. Before I could work through the pain and contortions of the electric shock, Strong-arm acted on his own. His foot had somehow broken the shackle on the floor where we were both tied down; he reached up with his foot, and used all his remaining strength to kick me away from the table. My own simple leg restraints gave under the pressure as my seat flew backwards into the crowd. Strong-arm stood, arms raised over his head announcing his victory. His blood-stained smile waved in front of me like a flag, signaling my failure.

The crowd around us, however, didn't seem to approve of his success. While I still maintain there is no honor among thieves, there is a certain code in the underworld that rules the Dark Zones. Despite being in a roomful of rapists, murderers and the very worst that humanity had to offer, these men left no room for a cheater; not here. Not with the stakes as high as they were, or with the amount of physical pain each of us had suffered through. Grummold took a revolver from his jacket, and placed its muzzle to Strong-arm's forehead. Without a word of warning, he pulled the trigger, splattering Strong-arm's brains across the already bloodthirsty crowd. Placing his revolver back in his jacket, Grummold took the gavel in his hands, and with one final swing toward the table, announced, "Sold for four-hundred thousand credits."

Grummold's men helped me up from where I'd landed as the crowd quickly dispersed. Walking up to the auctioneer, I held out a plastic card that he ran through a swipe machine. He keyed in six hundred thousand credits, and turned the device toward me.

"I bid four-hundred thousand, Grummold." I said, letting the dryness of my throat add a degree of deepness to my voice. "What's the extra two hundred K for? Killing Strong-arm?"

Grummold smiled and chuckled quietly as his men removed the body from the room.

"Hardly. If I had allowed him to cheat, I'd be either dead, out of business, or both in a matter of hours. The extra is my fee, of course; fifty percent of the winning bid."

"Isn't that supposed to be between you and the seller?" I asked, as I nonchalantly entered the numeric sequence to approve the transaction.

"Not this time," he replied, offering no explanation. Grummold then motioned toward the stage, saying "OK - they're all yours. Don't wear them out in one night!" They were cornered in a small, wheeled cage, and despite their silence, I could see they were truly terrified. I opened my backpack to retrieve my comm unit and place it back into my ear; leaving it in during the bidding would have shorted it out, and I knew I'd need it in order to get out of the Zone alive, let alone with my recent 'purchase' intact.

I bent down to the cage, and peered through the narrow aluminum bars. They each wore flimsy, threadbare nighties that had probably been white at some time in long forgotten past. "You could've at least cleaned them up a bit," I spat at Grummold. The two small sets of eyes in the cage looked at me fearfully, getting as far to the back of the cage as possible while still holding onto each other. I bent down to the cage again, and flashed the girls a broad smile.

"It's okay, loves - we're going to have a lot of fun! But first, you need a bath." I winked at the girls, then turned back to face Grummold. "You tell your customer that if they aren't up to snuff, I'm coming for him."

"That would be most unwise," Grummold shot back. "Nor would it be wise to seek me out... unless, of course, I have other items for you to procure for your pleasures."

If I didn't know it would blow my cover, I would have shot Grummold in the balls right then and there, but I couldn't afford the luxury of vengeance upon this filthy thing that called himself a man. It had taken me four weeks to penetrate the

Zone enough to even get close to this auction. God knows how many others like this would take place; but this one was unique. *'Twin girls, aged four years - living dolls for all your pleasures!'* the message had read. It was special even in the underworld of human trafficking, to have twins available for purchase, let alone some this young. Sadly, there were too many people who would've bought these girls for sick sexual gratification, torture, snuff films, or any one of a thousand horrors the depraved things around me called entertainment. The bankcard I had used would, of course, end up transferring no money to the criminals; the FBI was not in the habit of paying people like Grummold for little girls. Now, as I pushed the wheeled cage out of the room, and turned on my non-federal issue night vision glasses, I made my way out of the light of the room and into the deep unyielding night of Miami's Dark Zone. The sweltering heat of South Florida made this place feel more like a convection oven, and clothing was either limited or optional on the streets of the Zone. For my own part, the black dye that covered my naturally red curls only served to make me feel the heat more; add to that the deep olive skin dye that concealed the paleness of my Celtic heritage, and I felt like I was roasting alive.

The girls were sobbing softly in the cage, and I stopped just long enough to cover it with a thin sheet and give them each a pouch of cold water I had kept for them in my pack. As I did so, I leaned down and whispered to the girls, "My name is Ellie; I'm here to save you."

****

If anyone thought that the Dark Zone in Mobile, Atlanta, St. Louis or any other major American city was the worst thing they'd ever seen, you knew automatically they'd never been to the Zone in Miami. This place was unlike any other; not only was the humidity almost unbearable, but the concrete above acted like the walls of a brick oven. Add in the regular flooding during hurricane season, an overflow of Caribbean illegals, and the crime controlled industries that still interacted with the world above, and arguably you had the most dangerous mix of drugs, money, and free access anywhere in the world. The streets of the Miami Dark Zone were always packed with people, almost all of whom were criminals in one or more countries. With the Port of Miami being directly connected to the far edge of the Zone, there was essentially a full featured port of access, allowing anything from Opium and weapons, to biochemical stockpiles of medical waste and human slaves to move freely into and out of the US. The Crime Lords ran free here in Miami, letting their industries take complete advantage of the unbridled access in the Zone, all while having 'civilized lives' above in the comfort of the new city.

It was only a matter of time before my deceit would be discovered. Grummold was sure to be more than a little upset when he learned that the money transfer was a fraud, and if I wasn't out of the Zone with the girls by then, I may not make it out at all.

"Zim," I said softly after tapping the control switch in my pocket to activate the comm in my ear. "I've got the girls - now get us out of here."

"That may not be as easy as I'd like, Ellie," Zim answered nervously. "According to the bank capture we used for you to buy them, the transaction reversal is starting now, and I can't stop it. You off the main street yet?"

I took a look around and saw an alleyway that looked unoccupied. "Will be in two seconds, Zim." I made my way over to the entrance of the alleyway, pushing the girls along the rough and uneven road in the hybrid cart/ cage. "I can't wait to get you two out of there." I said, directing my voice toward them.

"But we've got to get out of this place first, ladies."
The girls sat in their cage, snuggling a dirty, stuffed
rabbit between them. One of the girls looked to the
rabbit, then over at her sister, who turned her head to
face me. She grabbed the back of the rabbit's neck
and it nodded an approval for them all.

The alleyway was almost abandoned, save for
a few men and boys slumped against the walls in a
drug-induced fog. I went in as deep as I could go,
staying as far away from the people here as was
physically possible. "All right, Zimmerman," I
asked, speaking into the air. "How do we get out of
here?"

I could hear Zim's fingers darting across his
keyboard, his usual rhythm upset by his nervousness.
"OK, Ellie. You are about two miles from the
waterfront. Michaels is headed to Pier 23 with a boat
and can pick you up there. You just have to get
there."

"Sounds too easy, Zim. What's the catch?" I asked,
finding myself pacing around my new cubs like a
lioness waiting for battle.

"You have to go back the way you came, El."
Zim said.

"You mean I've got to skirt around Grummold?" I asked. The mention of his name made the girls whimper in their vessel, and attracted some unwanted attention from a man who had entered the alley from the other side. "You've got to be kidding me, Zim." I groaned, turning the cart around and reaching in it to stroke the girls' heads with my fingertips. I took a deep breath. "So back the way I came. How good is your fix on my position?"

"Fuzzy at best, Ellie. But I did manage to hack into some of the old security cameras scattered around the zone. I used a modified recovery drone to repair a few of them, so I can at least tell you that you currently have a pretty clear path to the waterfront."

"You're a God-send, Zim." I left the channel open as I made my way back out into the street, and worked to get my bearings to find the waterfront. The smell of human waste and filth kept me from using my nose to find the water. All I could do was look out into the green-tinged darkness to find the silhouettes of buildings I had come to know during my stay here.

I almost wish that I could have been a fly on the wall when Grummold discovered my deceit. Not only would I have been able to witness the fruits of my labor, but it would have given me notice that he had indeed discovered the bogus money transfer. If I had known that, I could have guessed on precisely how much time I had to get the girls and myself past his little corner of the Zone. One thing is for certain; I definitely would have been a lot more careful rounding the corners of the old warehouse district, and possibly have been more prepared for the gunfire that erupted in my direction. The girls let out startled screams while bullets jetted by, and I jerked their cage back around the corner for a moment of safety, quickly loosing the gunmen in the maze of old warehouses and broken shipping containers that created the skyline here.

"Shh.... it's OK girls." I said, stooping low so they could hear me over the gunshots. "I'm gonna sneak us out of here; but I need you two to be really really quiet, alright?" Once again the smaller of the two girls looked to the rabbit, then to her sister, who looked to the stuffed rabbit and had it nod their approval. I smiled a broad, friendly smile for them, and stood back up, draping the sheet over their cage and began to work my way behind the building.

Pier 23 was the best and worst choice for our escape. I knew that, as the old dock closest to the real business ports, we had the advantage of possible backup, more than a hint of sunlight, and lots of water. While all that sounded good, it came with a price. Pier 23 was also the bottleneck for getting things in and out of the Zone by water. As such, crime families from across the globe had representation here, to look out for their own interest. Sadly, it was also the most logical place for an escape. If I was lucky, I could use that to my advantage. If my luck had finally run its course, not as much as a finger of mine would ever see its way out of the Zone.

****

The shadow of New Miami covered the old wharf district both literally and figuratively. As part of its design, New Miami had support columns well out into the water, causing the waterfront to be a mix of silhouettes, blinding rays of distant sunlight, and almost opaque darkness. The wheels of the girls' cage squeaked slightly over the rough, worn pavement, and we rolled along the backside of the first of the warehouses until we found an unlocked door. I gently drew it open and found the inside of the 'abandoned' warehouse to be a busy hub of activity. In the center of the large open room, six large trucks were parked; their cargo areas open and a few dozen men switching large boxes between them. Since all of these places were supposed to be shut down more than a decade ago, you could guarantee that whatever packages these folks were processing were far from legal. No matter what they were doing, they weren't paying us any attention, and I wanted to keep it that way. My only goal right now was to get the girls out of here alive, and we quietly made our way around the activities in the center of the warehouse, and over to a door on the other side of the building.

We were able to make it through six more warehouses in this fashion; each one bringing us closer to Pier 23. When the girls and I entered the last warehouse, just outside our escape point, I immediately knew it was going to be different. The trucks in this warehouse were carrying weapons - lots of weapons. Another truck rolled in through the front bay, and more armed men jumped out, pointing their guns at the crew who was already present. I thought to myself, *"Damn it, Ellie; why did you pick this warehouse to cut through?"* The two groups of men shouted and made racial slurs at each other, raising the chance of a firefight. The terms 'Reeferistas' seemed to be thrown out at the men who sported large, pot-leaf shaped tattoos on their necks. These men in turn called out the 'Listillios', who each wore orange and purple tops decorated with anything from braids of hair to baby toys. As the men argued and waved their firearms around, the girls and I tried our best to get to the large open bay door that bordered the pier we needed. Just as we made our way behind a stack of containers near the corner of the front wall, Grummold walked into the warehouse with a team of gun wielding henchmen behind him.

The old saying of 'shoot first and ask questions later,' seems to be a rule of thumb in the Dark Zones. Upon seeing an armed mass enter their already flaring argument, both sets of men in the center of the warehouse started shooting at Grummold and his men, who in return opened fire. Before I knew what was happening, more men started coming down ladders and jumping down from above in the warehouse, increasing the number of bullets two-fold. I took the opportunity to slowly back our way to the door we'd come though, whispering to the girls, "Let these boys play their little games. While they play cowboys and Indians, we'll sneak around from behind them!" The girls looked up at me blankly for a moment, then a small smile spread across both their faces.

I still say it was as good a plan as any we could've put together, given the situation. I knew Michaels would be waiting for me by now, so all I had to do was get to the end of the pier. With the firefight happening behind us, I really didn't think that anyone would be looking around for me. My boss, Director Forrest, said in my last review that I didn't make a lot of mistakes, but when I did, they were usually doozies. In hindsight, this was definitely a doozie. We tried our best to sneak past the building in the blossoming twilight of the Zone, but when we got to the pier, we discovered that Grummold was one step ahead of us. Pairs of armed men jumped up from the sides of the pier where they'd been waiting for me. The gunfire behind us subsided, and soon the girls and I were surrounded on the old wooden dock, the muzzles of dozens of high velocity machine guns pointed right at us.

The girls huddled more closely together in their cage, trying to press their way through the wire bars to somehow touch me for comfort or protection. I reached down and stroked their hair as best as I could while the thugs around us tightened their circle. There was no way we could run through together for an escape, and there was no way I was going to let these girls go while I had a breath in my body.

"Six-Hundred Thousand is a lot of money to steal from me, little girl." Grummold said as he stepped through the barrier of guns that encircled the girls and I. "Add to it that you took merchandise you didn't pay for, and I am very cross with you." He gestured toward the girls, stating, "We'll just have to put these back up for sale. As for you, maybe we can find a buyer for you too!" Grummold reached out toward me to grab my arm, but pulled his hand back with a yelp before he ever touched me. Just as I felt the wood beneath my feet start to give way, the end of Grummold's forefinger fell off, leaving a cauterized wound where it had been attached moments before. The unmistakable hum of a high-yield laser reached my ears from the water below us, and whatever bits of wood or fate had held us up finally gave way, sending the girls and I screaming downward into the sewage-filled waters of the Port of Miami. I held the girls' cage tightly, yelling, "Take a deep breath, girls! We're almost out!" Only a few seconds passed before we crashed into the water, surrounding us in filth and the momentary silence of the sea. As we bobbed back to the surface, a speedboat piloted by Michaels came charging up to us, and using a miniature loading arm to scoop us out of the water, deposited us into the bow. Bullets started raining down from the old wharf above us, putting multiple holes in the borrowed rescue boat Michaels had acquired. While I struggled to get my bearings I took a glancing shot to the upper arm, sending fire through my body as the putrid water ate away at the open flesh. Michaels did his best to focus on maneuvering the rescue boat in a zigzag pattern to make us harder to hit. The soaked girls huddled together in their cage, whimpering in each other's arms and holding the tattered stuffed rabbit between them.

I yelled out "Pulser!" to Michaels. Despite the vagueness of the one-word command, he knew exactly what I needed, and tossed my cherry red Pulser to me. I sat up past the buzzing bullets, the rich red flow of my blood dripping down my arm, and started unloading a volley of my own on the loathsome group behind us. The sound waves from the Pulser blasts knocked most of them to their knees, and allowed me to target the decaying supports of the old wooden dock we'd just escaped. It started to crack and crumble just as Michaels hit the edge of the shadows around us, maneuvering the speedboat out of the Dark Zone.

For the first time in almost a month, I felt the warm sunlight paint itself across my bare shoulders. The night vision goggles switched themselves off immediately, and I tossed them aside and into the open ocean so I could see the blue sky. The boat threw a mist of water across the girls and I, offering me the first bath I'd had in weeks, and I immediately dropped my weapon and reached over to open the top of the cage the girls had called home for far too long. The smaller of the two struggled out first, as her sister passed their rabbit up to her, and pushed upward on her bottom to lift her out of the cage and into my arms. I sat the first girl in my wet lap, and reached over to help the second girl out as well.

While Michaels took us to the safety of a Coast Guard Cutter just offshore, the girls sat, one of each knee, with their tiny arms wrapped tightly around me, their rabbit and each other.

2
❦Whispers❧

Five hours had passed, and the girls hadn't said a word, either to us, or to each other. The Coast Guard Cutter Gallatim had provided us with emergency medical services, sterilizing my wound and giving the girls a quick once-over. They dropped us off after an hour at sea, and Michaels and I took the girls to Miami Central for a much needed and more thorough checkup. Director Forrest had made sure that a team of Bureau doctors were ready and waiting when we arrived. Despite their silence, the girls each protested with kicks and shrill, panicked screams when the nursing staff tried to lead them away from me. Looking at the girls' eyes, there was no way I could possibly walk away from them, or put them through a moment of worry or distress that wasn't absolutely necessary. I knelt down, taking their small hands in mine, and said, "Don't worry loves; I'm right here." I looked up at the impatient nurses and added, "…and I'm not going anywhere."

Each of the girls had a full body scan followed by a physical exam. I helped them shower and change into hospital gowns afterwards. I felt like a weight had been lifted off my soul when the doctors told me they had not been sexually assaulted. We couldn't rule out other types of abuse; hell, just what they witnessed during the auction counted as emotional abuse. All we could do now was wait to make sure they had no diseases, check their scans for tracer implants and wait for them to talk.

The girls didn't want to let me out of their sight, so I left the bathroom door open to the hospital room while I showered, making sure I constantly talked to them. While under the hot water, I washed several weeks' worth of grime and nastiness out of my hair, along with the black dye I'd used to hide my appearance. The girls' eyes lit up when I came back into the hospital room, my bright fire-red hair almost glowing against the white robe Michaels had brought up for me earlier. They sat together on their bed, play-whispering to the rabbit and seeming to communicate between themselves with only a look and a glance. Still, I talked to them, about toys and cartoons, food and ponies - anything I could think of to try and help these girls begin the process of healing. I could tell they were listening to me, but no force on earth could make them respond before they were ready to.

A soft knock on the door made the girls jump and huddle together on the bed.

"It's okay, loves." I said, reaching out to calm them. I called back to the door saying, "It's open." all the while keeping an eye on my Pulser on the dresser, just in case.

Michaels entered the room, carrying a large shopping bag. "I didn't wake them, did I Ellie?" he asked, setting the bag down next to me on my bed.

"No, Aaron. We're just sitting here talking. Did you bring the Melacin?" I asked. Michaels nodded with a smile, reaching into the bag and handing me a small bottle and a container full of what looked like baby wipes. "Excellent! I want my old skin back." The girls looked at each other curiously, but still spoke not a word. I took the lone pill in the bottle that Michaels had brought to me, chasing it with cold water from the bedside dispenser. "What's the transition time, Aaron?" I asked, opening up the wipes and pulling one out.

"The Melacin in the pill will take a few hours to clear out the colour from your scalp and other places, Ellie, but according to Forrest, these wipes should work pretty much on contact."

I stood up with an excited bounce in my step, giving Michaels a quick slug to the chest and a smile as I walked past him to the dresser in the small hospital room. Removing the chemical-soaked wipes, I started cleaning my face with them. With each swipe the olive toned skin dye started to come off, revealing my freckled complexion underneath. As I wiped away the disguise, the wide-eyed girls both got down off their bed and moved to stand next to me. They watched intently for several minutes as I uncovered my face, neck and arms. I looked down at the little girls, and said, "It's kind of like makeup, loves; but this stuff won't wash off in water." I instructed, pointing to a swath of colour on my skin. "I have to use these wipes to make it all come off." I knelt down to them, and tagged them each on the nose with the cloth, crinkling my own nose and grinning as I did so.

"Hey kids." Michaels said, startling the girls into a fright. They scrambled into my arms, whimpering, and I looked back to Aaron.

"Shhh, Shh. Hold on, loves." I said to the girls. "This is my friend, Aaron. He helped me rescue you. He's a friend, loves; I swear he won't hurt you; not ever." The girls relaxed just a tad in my arms as they pretended to whisper to their fabric rabbit. After a few minutes of uncertainty, the rabbit was made to slowly nod an approval, and the girls got down from my arms and went back to their bed. They both sat starring at Michaels now, still not saying a word.

"Um, well." Michaels stammered, speaking softly, afraid to scare the little girls again. "I just thought that you ladies would be more comfortable in something nicer than hospital gowns, so I went down to the store and bought you each some clothes." With this, he moved his shopping bag gently over to the bed where the girls sat, and just as gently moved away. "I hope you like them." The girls, sitting side by side and holding the rabbit between them, each reached into the bag and pulled out pink and purple jerseys, running pants, and simple shoes. There was also a pack of clean undies (complete with stars and rainbows), socks and two candy bars each.

"Do you like those, girls?" Michaels asked. Once more, the girls conferred in pretend whispers with their shared stuffy, who was made to nod 'yes' with almost no hesitation. "I am so glad. I'm gonna step out of the room while you ladies get changed. Ellie," Michaels added, turning toward me as he left, "Thank you. I'll see you downstairs whenever you're ready."

It was getting dark outside when the girls received the "all clear" from their tests. With the overburdened healthcare system, we were quickly escorted out of our shared room, and down to a waiting vehicle that Forrest had sent for us. The black van slipped itself easily into traffic and soon we were on the Safeway heading towards New Miami. From there we'd head to the Federal Building, and into a two-room apartment set up for special situations. While we zipped along toward what would be our home for the night, the girls fell asleep, one on each side of me. I couldn't help but think that it was the soundest sleep they'd had in a very long time.

****

3
❧Identity❧

Zim had spent the night working his magic to dig up info on the girls. We had gotten their DNA at Miami Central, and Zimmerman grabbed it and ran, as he was known to do. Before my alarm even went off, Zim was buzzing me on my comm, excitedly spitting out the information he'd managed to round up.

"Erin and Olivia Carter – born January 26th, 2051 to Madeline Francis Carter." Zim excitedly offered as I picked up the line. "Birth records say their biological father is a man named Julian Sheldon; he lives here in Miami."

I sat up sleepily, holding my comm in one hand and rubbing my eyes with the other. The girls each lay on the bed next to me, gently sleeping with the dirty stuffed rabbit still held between them.

"Okay Zim. So I take it we know where to find the girl's parents, then?" I whispered, gently reaching over and touching the nearest of the girls on the arm.

"Well, that gets a little more complicated, Ellie. According to Miami's Recovery drone records, their mother was found dead over a month ago in the zone. DNA didn't hit any active cases, so the little guy did what he was built to do. Their mom is literally dust in the wind now."

"What about their father?" I inquired, reaching over to gently move hair out of the smaller girls' face. "This Sheldon guy. What do we have on him?"

A small *'hrmph'* echoed across the comm line, and I could hear the click-clack of Zim's keyboard in the background. "Looks like he has a history of petty theft and smuggling as a teen, then Police records on him stop until last summer. Tax records show a windfall around five years ago that reportedly made him pretty wealthy. Court records show a shared custody between the mother and father."

"What happened last summer?" I inquired. Zim sent a signal to the comm terminal in the main room, and I moved away from the sleeping girls into the early morning light of the small living area to see what Zimmerman had uncovered. I quickly scanned the new data Zim had populated on the screen, and felt my stomach lurch as I read over the file.

"A rape case? You mean their father raped their mother? Then how the hell did he get joint custody?"

"He countersued, Ellie. The local papers seemed to think the case was fixed, but the girls' mother could never prove rape. After he was acquitted, he had more than enough evidence to prove paternity, and the court ordered his name be added to the birth records. They also ruled that the parents share custody, although I show nothing that says the girls have ever lived with him. Plus, he hasn't filed a missing persons report on them; I doubt he has a clue that their mother is dead, or that the girls were almost sold off."

"My ass he doesn't know." Zim sat quietly on the other end of the comm, waiting for me to finish the inevitable rant he knew was about to ensue. "Any parent would know if their kids were out of contact for a month or more. And if he doesn't know, that's just another reason to make sure he doesn't take the girls home."

"You going with the deadbeat dad approach, Ellie?" Zim asked. "Cause if you are, it's going to be hard to prove. He's got trust funds set up for each of the girls at Federal banks around the country. The courts usually look to the parent the kids live with to check on negligence; the secondary parent is judged more on what they do for the kids monetarily - and this guy's got that covered."

I looked over to the open bedroom door and saw the girls cuddling with each other, barely stirring in the early morning light that danced into the room between the curtains. "This Sheldon guy doesn't feel right, and I can't just turn these girls over to someone without..."

"Ellie, you may have to." Zim sent a new file over to me for review. "When I made a match on the girls ID, I hit some sort of flag in the Miami system. From what I can see, it looks like someone in the Miami PD has already informed him that his daughters have been found. He could show up any time."

"Then start digging, Zim." I pled. "Dig fast and dig hard."

****

Part of me wanted to spend the morning, or as long as it took, on the comm in the room trying to find any reason to not let Julian Sheldon just waltz in and take these children. As much as that felt like a driving force to my day, I knew the girls needed my direct attention and I knew that Zim was working hard and fast to find a way to help me keep them safe. I put aside the computer and went into the tiny kitchen to make the girls some breakfast.

When the smell of eggs and pancakes started filling the room, I heard them stir in the bedroom. They filed out, sleepily rubbing their eyes and still dragging the rabbit between them.

"Good morning my loves!" I called to the girls as they approached the table. "I thought a nice breakfast would be a great way to start your day today.   Who   wants   pancakes?"

Both girls smiled at each other, then looked to their rabbit, who raised his arms up in the air. I finished plating up a neat short stack and placed it on the table, adding scrambled eggs and milk for each of the girls, and sat down to finish filling their plates for them.

****

It was almost nine A.M. when Michaels called me. He had been downstairs in the labs running test on everything that had been retrieved from the girls at Miami Central. The news he gave me pissed me off more than Zimmerman's news about the girls' father. The Bureau doctors Forrest had sent to examine them had taken plenty of infrared and sub-dermal photographs, looking for trace evidence of any kind. Michaels said these photos showed the girls had been repeatedly beaten, probably with wet towels filled with beans, soap or some other malleable implement to keep them from bruising. He shuffled a few of the pics to the terminal in front of me as the girls played silently on the floor.

"You can see from the infrareds that there are large swaths of areas on the back, legs and the cheeks of both girls that would normally have bruised. Considering the colouration, these span a period of time from over 4 weeks old to as recent as two days ago."

35

"That partially explains why they were so jumpy yesterday, Aaron." I said, looking down at them playing silently with the once white rabbit. "And the psychological trauma explains why they haven't talked to any of us yet."

"Yup. They're still terrified, and very unsure of what is going to happen next. My best guess would say that if anyone is likely to get through to them, it will be you, Ellie." Michaels paused again, then asked, "Have you asked them which one is which yet? Zim told me he found out their names."

"Nope; but now is as good a time as any. I'll buzz you back." I hit the control on the comm to end the conversation, and went to sit with the girls on the floor.

"Did you ladies enjoy breakfast?"

The girls looked to the rabbit, who was made to rub his tummy as they each licked their lips. "OK. Good." I crossed my legs and added, "My friend Zim looked at the blood they took from you at the hospital last night. He looked at it, and he saw all the little tiny things that live in your blood, and those little things told him your names."

36

The rabbit shook his head no.

"No, he really did." I held out my hand to wordlessly ask for the rabbit. "I bet if I whispered your names to him, he'd let me know if I was right; wouldn't he?" The girls looked at each other, furrowing their brows. After a moment, the larger of the two timidly handed the stuffed rabbit to me. I held him up and whispered quietly in his ear, then took my hand to turn his head back to look at the girls, then back to me to nod yes.

I handed the rabbit back to the now wide-eyed girls in front of me. "I'm gonna say your names are Olivia and Erin. Am I right?" Both girls nodded in agreement, taking turns to look at the battered toy rabbit they once again held between them. Each of them had shown a physical response as I said their names, so I now knew which one was which.

"Do either of you remember who I am?" I asked. They both nodded yes, then Olivia, the smaller of the two, quietly answered, "Ellie", then threw up her arms as though she expected to be hit for speaking.

****

4
❦Downfall❧

It would be another two days before we heard from Julian Sheldon. During that time, I worked with Erin and Olivia, playing games, reading stories, and trying to gently pry more words from them, while Michaels and Zimmerman kept plugging away on the case. We knew that the girls' story would never be admissible in court due to their age, but if we could corroborate their story with evidence, we wouldn't need to rely on the words of two emotionally traumatized four year olds. As much as I felt these girls would be a gold mine of information, it would be science that would be the key to stopping the trafficking in the Dark Zone.

While I had been in the Zone, I had taken advantage of the darkness and used a portable E-MRI scanner to grab as much detail from the auction room as I could. As I had sat in the torturous 'bidding machine', watching Grummold get his jollies from my physical agony, the cylindrical device sat concealed in my backpack, casting an invisible net over the entire crowd. When the Holo-recreator digested the data and started spitting out faces from the crowd, our friends at the Miami PD were somewhat surprised to find that more than a few of the men and women from the auction were well-known locals; people that had been previously thought to be upstanding citizens, politicians and religious leaders. Since it was illegal to even try to buy or sell another human being, their very presence at the auction sealed their fates, and soon the local police were rounding up these charlatans and charging them with human trafficking. Sadly, after only three arrests, the other half-dozen people recognized from the Zone simply vanished. Even though they may have been hiding with their cohorts underneath New Miami, penetrating the zone for a handful of arrests was impractical, to say the least.

While the local scandal broke over these few individuals, Zimmerman worked to recreate the scene from the auction room E-MRI scan. If we'd been in our office in Mobile, he could have used his modified equipment to upload the data and create the data web in less than a day, but the equipment here in Miami was outdated even by most Federal standards. Since their holo-recreator wasn't set up for full interaction, the best we could do would be to go in, and look for things I'd missed.

The Miami Federal Offices were actually built into a portion of the raised foundation of New Miami. Many of the Governmental buildings here were literally carved into the acres of concrete and steel that held up mile upon mile of the new city. Their construction made these offices Hurricane and Disaster proof. Were a Tsunami to hit the coast of Florida, the Zone underneath the city would be wiped out, but all the infrastructure needed for recovery would still be intact. It was a brilliant piece of engineering, but had the effect of making many of the Offices in Miami very small, dark, and cave-like.

In Mobile, our Holo-recreator was top-notch, even before Zimmerman started making his 'special' modifications. Here, the Holo-recreator was an add on, and it looked every bit the afterthought. What had been planned as a conference room had been converted into their Holo-recreator. The tiny space had multiple grids laid out in a hound's-tooth pattern on the walls, ceiling, and floor, with two computer terminals on each wall. A secondary generator had been placed in the room to help power the old unit. Had there not been a sound-proof dome covering the extra generator, there was no way we could have handled the noise of it running endlessly in the small, enclosed space.

"Let's get this over with, boys," I said as Michaels, Zimmerman and I opened the door to the recreated vision of the Auction room from the zone. Were it not for the lack of smell or movement, the visual recreation would have been all too convincing. Everything from the cracks in the old cinderblock walls to the beads of sweat on Grummold's brow was a perfect snapshot of a single moment.

Michaels walked to the middle of the room, passing right through the ghostlike crowd and strode up to the image of me sitting at the bidding machine.

"You look like Hell, Ellie," he said, pointing out the contortions that were frozen on the image of my face.

"It was worth it to get them out of here," I answered, pointing over to the small stage at the holographic girls, frozen and horrified in their cage. "And I'd do it again if I had to."

As Michaels and I walked around the table where Strong-arm and I were both 'bidding' for the

41

girls, Zim was going through the crowd and removing figures as they were identified. After only a few minutes of this, he had the crowd pared down to only a dozen unknown attendees. Four of these faces hit from an international criminal database, but the last eight were unidentifiable.

Shifting my attention, I moved to place myself behind Grummold. On his makeshift podium, I could see papers that documented the sale of the girls; my heart sank when I remembered the limitations of the Holo-recreator here in Miami. Had we been in our home office, I could have literally picked up the light-based paper to read it. As it was, all I could make out was the names of the girls, and part of a local address.

"That bastard knew who they were!" I shouted, wanting to scream and howl. Michaels came around and looked at what I was seeing, and he too started to get angry.

"What is this local address Ellie?" he asked, trying to stay focused. "All I can make out is the Miami zip code."

"Then we search that zip for anyone with any connection to the girls." I took my camera and flashed a shot of the paper under Grummold's elbow, focusing on the portion of an address that hung before us like a carrot.

****

Michaels and I spent the rest of the day trying to gather evidence and take interviews from the people involved in Sheldon's rape trial. It didn't take us long to find a common theme: all the jurors were either missing, or had left town to destinations unknown. A couple of them had turned up dead in the Dark Zone. By four-thirty that afternoon Michaels and I had exhausted the list of jurors, legal assistants and court officers. Aside from the judge himself, there were only two people we could try and talk to: the prosecuting attorney and the defense attorney.

Autumn C. Anderson was well known in the South-eastern circuit court. She had a knack for defending the poor, especially women, and taking on her adversaries with a gusto that rivaled a military general. Once you were in Autumns' sights, you were pretty much done for. Julian Sheldon's was one of the few cases she had ever lost.

We sat in her office in New Miami. The building was close to the Federal Building, on the eastern side of town. The style and design of the office was very art deco, with elaborate wall panels and decorated ceilings you could stare at for hours. Autumn sat behind her desk, her bouffant hairstyle harkening back to an era long past, and lit a cigarette as she began shuffling through files on her terminal.

"Yup –thought that one was a slam dunk, agents." She said as she forwarded files to my handheld. "Here you had a guy who had never even met my client before her rape, and you had DNA in the form of those lovely little girls that said he had fathered them. There was a rape kit on file at Miami Central documenting the assault, and witnesses placed Sheldon at the store she was found behind right before and after the attack. It was open and shut."

"Then what happened, Ms. Anderson?" Michaels asked, injecting himself into the discussion.

"You tell me. All the evidence went missing; some sort of 'clerical error' at the police department. When it was found, the evidence seals had been compromised, and it was all deemed inadmissible. Even the video footage of him following my client through the store was found to have been," she paused, reading directly from a court file, " 'digitally

44

tampered with and thus inappropriate for use in the judicial system'. I personally took that footage to the FBI labs at Quantico, and they couldn't find as much as a pixel that displayed any sign of tampering."

"So the judge was bought off, then?" I offered. Autumn sat back in her chair and breathed a deep sigh before she spoke.

"If he was, they did a damn good job of hiding it. I took the risk of having him investigated by 'private means', and they found nothing. But with the evidence tampering and video being ruled inadmissible, all we had was DNA and hearsay testimony. All DNA proved was that he was the girls' father; and we both know any damn fool can father a child. Ms. Carter was devastated; more so when her rapist turned around and sued her for parental rights and custody."

"What about the jurors, Ms. Anderson?" Michaels asked, continuing "We couldn't find anyone left in town that served on that jury. Any ideas about what happened there?"

"Probably paid off, scared off, or shut up, depending on their reactions to being threatened or bribed. Sheldon's had run-ins with the law for almost twenty years, and he's only thirty four. He knows the system, and he has the money to work with the best at being the worst."

Autumn started checking her comm, and I had a feeling there was either nothing more we would get from her, or simply nothing more she had to offer us. I stood first, thanking her for her time as Michaels and I headed for the door. Just before we reached the doorway, I turned around and asked one more question of her. "One last thing, Autumn; why do you think you weren't bribed or threatened?"

At this, Autumn sat back down and turned her attention to her terminal. Her only answer was, "Who said I wasn't? I'm sorry, but there is nothing more I can do to help you."

****

I thought I knew what responsibility was. As an FBI agent, I was responsible for my team; I was responsible for any case I was on as well as for enforcing the laws that our society and Government had put in place. As heavy a weight as that had been from time to time, nothing in my life had even begun to prepare me for the responsibility I felt for Erin and Olivia. When the boys and I went into the holo-recreator for a few hours, I had left knowing that the girls would be in a safe, almost preschool-like environment. Later, when I returned from the wild goose chase Michaels and I had undergone, I was stopped at the door by one of the local agents, a man named Gallindo whom I had met when we arrived in Miami over a month ago.

"Gallindo! Hey there," I said as he walked up to shake my hand. "How is everything?"

"Oh, pretty good Ellie. But I am glad you are done. Those girls you brought in have been crying their little heads off since you left them upstairs."

I was suddenly hit with a sinking feeling in my stomach; not the nervous exuberance of butterflies, or the sickening knot of tragic news. The only way I can describe it would be this: hearing the girls were so upset made me feel suffocated, and my fight response kicked in immediately. I myself was surprised to have this reaction, but all I could think of at the time was Erin and Olivia.

"Where are they?" I inquired, trying to hold my nervousness in check. "Is my boss with them? What are they doing? Are they hurt?" A sudden flood of fear driven questions came to mind, and before

Agent Gallindo could answer, a thousand possible horrors began playing in my head.

"They're in children's observation, level 32. I think Jim is there with them."

Gallindo's response was cut short in my head as I dashed for the lift to level 32, leaving Michaels and Zimmerman standing with him. I bounced nervously in the lift as it carried me upward to my girls, and ran straight into Director Forrest when the doors opened.

"Ellie, calm down." Jim said as he steadied me from our collision. "What's the rush?"

"Agent Gallindo said the girls had been crying and upset since I left," I responded, hearing how lame my reasoning sounded now that it was spoken aloud. I looked down the hallway, adding, "That's all." I struggled inside to regain my self-control before I continued. "I wanted to make sure they were alright."

"They're fine, Ellyandra. I spent most of the afternoon with them, and after I told them you were coming back soon, they settled down. They've been playing with that rabbit of theirs for the last few hours."

The very idea that the girls were hurting had put me into fight mode; now the news that they were fine was like a giant stone being lifted from my chest, and I found I could breathe again. Jim motioned to a nearby bench, and we both took a seat.

"Ellie, what's going on here? These aren't your girls; and you've worked with children before. I've never seen you react like this, and quite frankly it worries me."

I knew I had to choose my words carefully with Jim. He was a friend, but he was also my boss. If he thought I was losing control where the girls were concerned, I'd be off the case before I could sneeze.

"Sir, I saw the conditions those little girls were kept in back in the Dark Zone. They've been through too much already; I just ..."

"You want to keep them safe, Ellyandra." Jim interjected, finishing my thought. "But that is our job as a group, not yours alone. I know the girls have been through a lot; psychologically speaking, they have been traumatized in ways we can only imagine. But if you are going to help them, one of the first things they have to learn is that we are *ALL* trying to help them together."

I nodded my head, understanding exactly where he was coming from. "There's no way I can stay with them twenty-four seven to keep them safe, and do my job at the same time." I answered, only half-heartedly making the statement. "And they have to know that. Doing my job is the best way to keep them safe permanently."

"Exactly". Jim said as he stood, making a sweeping motion toward the hallway, "Now that we have that settled, I do believe you have a two member fan club waiting to see you."

5
❧Intervention❧

Julian Sheldon considered himself a man of the world. He thought he dressed well, and believed he commanded a presence in any room he stepped into. He entered the Federal Building in New Miami with a swagger that said he owned the place. His blazing white suit reflected the interior lighting so much that it almost hurt to look at him. Aside from his body language and expensive clothing, everything else about him screamed 'thug wanna-be' in every possible way. He wore his shirt opened to the navel, showing off his pale and less than formidable set of abs. He sported slicked-back, black-dyed hair that dripped with the amount of oil holding it down. He was gaudy and trashy, with a gold and diamond grill on his teeth from an era long passed, and awful, poorly-drawn tattoos on his exposed chest.

"Ey!" he yelled at the front desk clerk. "Are you blind? Can't you see I'm standin' here?" Mr. Sheldon paced back and forth in front of the reception desk, adding, "You got sumthin that belongs to me."

Michaels and I watched him on the video feed, and I felt nauseous thinking of him taking Erin and Olivia.

"Here I had hoped that people like this only existed in bad movies and pulp fiction." Michaels bemoaned. "And now here we are, getting ready to turn over Erin and Olivia to him. Just doesn't seem right."

"Two days after we know he was notified they were here, and *now* he finally shows up to get them?" I was doing a piss poor job of hiding my utter disdain for the man. "Nothing about this seems right, because none of this is right!" I clenched my fists tight, adding, "Quite frankly, the only thing that would make me feel the least bit good about this would be for me to forcibly put my foot up his..."

Director Forrest's timing cut me off mid-sentence as he entered the room where we were monitoring Julian Sheldon. His head was down, working madly on his pocket computer, and barely watching where he was going.

"Ellie", he said, barely acknowledging that we were even in the same room. "I need you to go upstairs and get the girls ready."

"Jim!" I began, but he cut me off immediately.

"Ellyandra: I need you to go upstairs, get the girls' things together, talk to them, and take about twenty minutes before you bring them down to the lobby. Do you understand me?" He stopped and looked me directly in the eyes as he said this, and I felt like a disobedient kid caught with her hand in the candy jar. All I could mutter out was a simple, "Yes, sir." Forrest immediately went back to whatever project he was running on his handheld, and I left him and Michaels in the low light of the observation room, solemnly heading toward the two room apartment the girls and I had shared for days now.

****

As much as I couldn't stand the idea, I didn't really have a choice. It took me a good ten minutes to get the girls calmed down, and another ten to get their little bags together. They had won the hearts of everyone here in the Miami office, and large amounts of clothes and toys had been brought in for the girls. I led the twins to the elevator, and they quietly marveled at the view as the glass lift plummeted down the side of the building. The rays of the sun were trying hard to beat down on New Miami, but a dark cloud kept moving its tendrils to keep a shadow cast over the city. As we rode down to the main floor, I hit the comm control in my pocket and asked, "Zim? You found anything yet?"

"Been pouring over Federal Statutes all morning Ellie, but I don't have a thing yet." he responded, his tone taking on an apologetic inflection.

"Thanks for trying Zim, but we're out of time. Talk to you soon."

The lift doors opened into the marble and steel hallway of the main floor, and the girls quietly held my hands as we walked toward the front door. Jim was waiting for me just around the corner, and the girls both drew close to me as he approached. I knelt down to them and gave them both big hugs before I spoke.

"OK my loves. Your father has come to take you home."

Erin looked to her sister, then back to me. "Our who?" she asked. I looked over my shoulder to Forrest, who was hanging his head and tapping relentlessly on his handheld computer.

"Your daddy, my dear."

I reached out to straighten Erin's top as Olivia answered, "We don't have a daddy, Ellie."

"We don't have a mommy either," Erin added. "Not anymore. Just Chester," she said, holding up the stuffed rabbit.

Around the corner, I could hear their 'father' yelling at the front desk officer, saying "Ey! I ain't got all day. I'm a busy man 'ere. Just bring da little brats 'ere and we'll go."

I took a picture of Julian Sheldon from my files and pulled it up on my handheld, showing it to the girls.

"Loves, have you seen this man before?" They both quietly shook their heads in a slow yes, then looked to the floor. My heart was pounding as the girls took my hands again, and Forrest led us around the corner.

Sheldon raised his arms up and yelled, "It's about frikkin time! Come on girls - we got places to go!" He signed a paper the front desk officer had held out for him, and acknowledged the signature with a thumbprint scan. As soon as the scanner beeped in acceptance of his ID, Sheldon reached out and yanked the girls away from me, giving me what my grandfather could only have called a *'Go to Hell'* look as he intentionally twisted their wrist into an obviously painful position.

"You did me good by findin them, " Sheldon said with a snarl. "Now don't bother us no more."

All I wanted to do was run to Erin and Olivia, but Jim held me fast by the arm as Sheldon took the girls and nearly drug them out of the building.

"Let   him   go,   Ellie."

I stopped struggling as my boss released me, reaching up to touch the comm in his left ear.

"OK Michaels. He's leaving the building now. We'll meet you out front."

I seized control of myself and turned to Forrest. "What are you up to, Jim?"

"Just doing my job, Ellyandra," Forrest answered, his broad smile finally coming through. "and my job says that his children were missing for over a month. While there are no Federal laws in place to cover this, there is an early 21st Century law here in Florida that I found about an hour ago. It was enacted after a mother had gone for a month without reporting her toddler missing. So now, primary custody in Florida does not release any parent - custodial or otherwise - from the responsibility of keeping a child safe."

"You set him up then," I responded, not sure if I wanted to punch my boss for keeping me out of the loop, or hug him for saving my girls.

"It almost didn't happen. I had to make sure that Caylee's law would hold up with all the statutes that have been passed since, but sure enough, I got word just after I sent you to get the girls that none of the new federal statutes, nor any more recent Florida laws would block it; I have Michaels waiting just outside to arrest him for child endangerment and negligence as soon as he walks out of the building."

6
❦Revelation❧

Arresting Julian Sheldon under Caylee's Law was admittedly a good feeling. I was afraid the charges wouldn't stick, and he'd be out on bail within the hour, but I also knew that as long as those charges were pending, even the Federal courts were powerless to turn the girls over to his care. Imagine how pleasantly surprised I was when I found the Court Office who had to set up the bail hearing was closed early due to a bomb threat. So like it or not, Julian Sheldon was destined to spend at least one night in jail, and I was going to do everything I could to help the girls recover from the 'near miss' of being turned over to him.

It looked like the two-room apartment in the Federal Building would be home for the girls and I for the next couple of days at least. I asked Michaels to run out and bring us some groceries so I could make dinner for us that night. My family's tradition of cooking as a way to bond was a little unconventional in child psychology, but it was the way I knew best. I couldn't have four-year-old girls chopping onions and prepping meats, but I could certainly sit them down on stools in the kitchen with me and talk with them as I made us a meal. My own memories of making meals with my family started this way, and even now over twenty-five years later, those memories brought me comfort and gave me a sense of well-being that I couldn't fully explain.

I decided to keep dinner simple; no shrimp etoufee, and no eleven course English dinners. I made roast chicken tenderloins, cheddar and garlic mashed potatoes, and macaroni and cheese. The girls sat quietly on step-stools in the kitchen as I cooked our meal, watching me intently while I boiled noodles, paid attention to cooking times and dashed seasonings across our fare. They were still very quiet, talking more to their stuffed rabbit Chester than to me; but they were here with me, not alone in some halfway house, or still stuck in the Dark Zone. And every time they started to say something to me, or ask about the 'dry green stuff I was putting on the food', it was a step in the right direction.

I pulled plates down from the small cupboard and placed them on the counter. While I was getting our dinner into serving bowls, I said "Erin, Olivia; can you girls take those plates to the table, please?"

Erin passed their rabbit to Olivia, and gently climbed down from her perch on the stool, gingerly reaching up for the plates, and pulling each down one by one to take them to the table. After three trips, the table was set. I danced around the girls, holding the platter of chicken over my head and making my way to the table. After I had delivered the last of the food, I went back into the kitchen to pick up Olivia, and reached down to take Erin's hand, allowing her to lead us to the dinner table. I waited until we had been eating for a little while before I asked them, "Loves, I have a question for you. You're not mad that Jim and Aaron took you back from Mr. Sheldon, are you?"

Olivia, her cheeks stuffed with Mac & Cheese, shook her head no. Erin did the same, then quietly added "He's not a nice man."

"How so, honey?" I asked, hoping to get something from the girls that I could use to help them. Erin was quiet, and looked over to her sister before filling her mouth with macaroni. Neither of the girls seemed willing to say why Sheldon was 'not nice', and I knew that if I asked them leading questions, they'd tell me exactly what they thought I wanted to hear. Since that wouldn't help anyone, I took another bite of my dinner, and let the topic drop.

There wasn't as much as a noodle of Mac & Cheese left from dinner; the same couldn't be said of the chicken or potatoes. Thankfully, I had never been one to be offended by leftovers. Before my friend Roberts died, he was the groups' garbage disposal, and anytime there was food remaining from a meal, we knew we could bring it all to Bobby and it would be gone in the blink of an eye. I chuckled to myself at the irony of that phrase, considering the events that led him to lose his eye and his life.

It's funny the things that bring memories from the background so close that you can feel the moments all over again. Something as simple as putting away leftovers suddenly had me back in the Dark Zone in Mobile, watching Bobby fight a madman to protect me. The voice of Erin shook me back to reality as she brought me three poorly balanced plates.

"You OK, Ellie?" she asked innocently. Olivia plodded along behind her, dragging Chester on the floor.

"I'm fine my loves." I said, kneeling down and reaching over to embrace both of them. "I was just remembering someone - someone who got hurt really bad trying to keep me safe." I held the girls close as I plopped down cross-legged on the kitchen floor, putting a kid on each knee.

Erin spoke first, asking in a very sad voice, "Did they die?"

"Yes, honey. He died protecting me."

Olivia reached around me, hugging me as tight as a four year old can, and began to cry softly. Erin reached over to stroke her sister's head, then joined her in embracing me.

"Oh loves, it's okay. I'm okay; there's no need to cry, girls." I gently said before I noticed Erin wasn't crying - only Olivia. The girls' soft hair pressed up under my chin as they snuggled in, one sister doing as much as she silently could to calm the tears of the other, while each of them held onto me for dear life. We sat for a while, just holding each other in a wordless, timeless moment. After a while, Olivia raised her little head, and wiped her eyes with my shirt. I couldn't help but laugh a bit as she did this, and she looked back at me with an expression that asked what was so funny. I kissed them both on top of their heads, and we moved into the living area to relax before bedtime.

****

Little girls are like small pieces of dynamite; they come prepackaged ready to create mayhem where ever they are placed; and after they have expended all their energy, what is left just lays around waiting to be moved. Erin, Olivia and I had played in the living area for at least two hours. Each moment spent with them gave them some semblance of what it was like to be a normal little girl, and what started out as a guessing game had somehow turned into a 'climb to the top of Ellyandra' sporting event. It wasn't long after our games had ended that Olivia curled up next to me and soon started sleeping soundly. Erin and I continued a quiet game of twenty questions, but soon she was yawning too, and I gently nudged her toward the bedroom while I picked up Olivia and carried her there.

I had to admit I was enjoying having these girls around. It had only been a couple of days, but already we had bonded on a level that I had only experienced with my family until now. Jim was right, of course. I had worked with children before, and as much as I loved them all, none had ever gotten as close to me as Olivia and Erin had. As I tucked Olivia into one side of the bed and leaned over to place my forehead on her cheek, Erin climbed into the bed on the other side. I placed Chester between them and pulled up the covers to tuck her in as well, then reached down to give my sleepy girl a hug.

"Ellie," she said quietly into my ear.

"Yes honey?" I pulled her back just enough to look her in the eyes and show her a big smile.

"Me and Livy wanna stay with you. Please don't make us go back to that stinky man."

I looked at her innocent eyes that were almost in tears. "Love, I may not have a choice. According to the law, he is your father, and you belong with him."

Erin took her sleeve and wiped a tear from her cheek as she laid down, saying only, "I unnerstan, Ellie. We're not yours, so you can't keep us."

"That's right my love. It would be like someone finding Chester," I said, reaching over to touch their prized possession, "and not wanting to give him back to you and Olivia."

"No it wouldn't Ellie," Erin said, half interrupted by a large yawn, "cause Stinky doesn't want to keep us anyway."

The investigator in my head wanted to start firing off a barrage of questions, but I held her in check, knowing that if I could be patient, what I needed to know was just around the corner. I could feel it in the pit of my stomach as I asked Erin, "Why would you say that my dear?"

"Cause he's the one that took us from mama." Erin paused, looking over to her sister, then added, "and he took us to the man who put us in the cage."

****

7
❧Sabot❧

The girls had been sleeping for several hours before the shock of Erin's revelation started to subside enough for me to even think about sleep. After Erin had drifted off, I had gone into the kitchen and stuffed a towel in my mouth so I could scream. Tears rolled down my cheeks while I screamed as loudly into the rolled-up towel as I dared without waking the kids. There were only a few things in this world that could make me this angry - and to me, seeing a parent willfully endanger their children was probably the worst thing anyone could ever do.

After I calmed down a bit, I walked back into the bedroom and watched the girls sleep. Every now and then Olivia would kick or quietly cry out, giving me small glimpses of the hellish dreams she likely didn't have the words to describe. Even in her sleep, Erin reached out for her sister each time, just gently holding her wrist, or making some other contact that seemed to calm Olivia back into a somewhat restful slumber. The girls' dark curls framed their faces perfectly, and even in their uneasy repose, they looked every bit the Angels I knew them to be. I watched over them, getting lost in my feelings for these sweet innocents, only to have the moment come crashing down as I remembered their father, and thought of the torment he was willing to sell his girls into - all for the love of money.

I don't know if I surveyed the girls for an hour, or for three, but I sat vacillating between a growing love of these children, and the purest hatred I had ever felt when I thought of their father. When Erin finally started twitching in her own nightmare, and I saw Olivia reach out her and start crying in her sleep, I made the decision that whatever it took, within the law or not, these girls would *never* go back to the man who tried to sell them.

The long night finally ended with a sunrise lost to me in waking dreams. I had probably dropped off for only a few hours, but oddly felt energized when I woke to the tug of small hands on my shirtsleeve. I opened my eyes to see Olivia holding the girls' stuffed rabbit up to my chest. Smiling, I reached out to bring her close, and the small girl crawled up next to me, burrowing into my personal space as though it were her own. As Erin slept next to us, we sat silently, watching the ever growing light outside our window, just holding each other as the day began.

****

Angry does not begin to describe the reaction my team had to Erin's revelation about her father. To say they were upset would be like calling the Greater Depression a minor correction in the market. After I took the girls downstairs to the in-house preschool, I met my team at a small coffee shop on the corner just outside the Federal building. While I relayed Erin's miserable tale, Director Forrest stayed quiet, holding back the flood of anger that turned his dark brown features a rich shade of purple. Zim sat shaking his head, tapping controls on his handheld while he listened.

Aside from the girls and myself, I was most concerned about Michaels. He held his tears in check, but clenched his fist so hard his hands started to bleed. I had known Aaron since we were children, and I knew things about his past that most people would never know. I knew he had married at eighteen, become a father at nineteen, and a widower at twenty. The loss of not only his wife, but also his baby daughter at the hands of a cannibalistic killer is what had prompted him to join me at the FBI, and caused him to focus on psychology and profiling. It made him an invaluable part of my team, as well as an old friend. Right now it also compromised his insight and learning, and added stress to the situation that Forrest and Zimmerman couldn't begin to understand.

Michaels stood up and half-screamed, tossing his hands in the air and looking like he *needed* to strike something. Just as I started to stand to help him re-gather his control, Zimmerman's voice broke the silence, hopping back into the conversation.

"Umh, Ellie? I think we don't have to worry about Mr. Sheldon anymore." he announced as he placed his handheld on the small table we were sharing.

"What happened Zim?" I paused, asking, "Did Hell freeze over last night?"

"No. Julian Sheldon was found dead in his cell this morning."

****

My mother had never been what one would call "religious". Neither was my grandfather; with his advancing age he'd become more spiritual than anything else. Regardless, I had been raised with a strong belief in always trying to do the right thing, and not wanting to cause harm or hurt to others. Even though it was hard to not be thankful for Julian Sheldon's death, I couldn't help but feel a little guilty for being so relieved to have him out of the picture. My girls were now safe from his reach, and that thought had me *almost* skipping down the hall toward the morgue. Still, that voice in my head kept saying, 'Be careful what you wish for Ellie - you just might get it'.

The morgue in the Miami Federal Building reminded me of the morgue at Police Headquarters in Mobile. It didn't have a holo-recreator, and looked like it hadn't seen as much as a fresh coat of paint since the nineteen nineties. One or two computer terminals and holo-monitors stood out starkly against the cold, baby blue ceramic tile that lined the floor, walls and ceiling. The room was mostly dark, with half the overhead lights either turned off or burned out. Doctors and assistants worked busily over bodies that had found their way here by means of everything from gunshots to vehicle crashes. Off to one side was the quarantine room, walled off with high impact glass and populated by men and women wearing what amounted to space suits, working on what had to be the remains of a six-hundred plus pound man. The office of the head coroner, Dr. Corbin, was set in the middle of the back wall, directly across from the main entrance. Dr. Corbin stood outside his small closet-like workspace, and beckoned for me to quickly join him. Before I could properly identify myself, he gently took me by the wrist and shuffled me into his office, quickly closing the door behind him.

"You must be Agent Dyett," he began, clicking the lock shut behind him. "I recognize your face from the Agent roster".

"I'm Dyett; why lock the door, Doctor?" I asked, my bottled -up joy quickly transmuting into an unease that I couldn't place.

"Just precautions. We do need to be quick though," he added, walking to his desk and grabbing a few data cards and scan sheets. "Never know when the walls will have ears".

I didn't get the chance to ask for an explanation. Dr. Corbin started hurriedly going through the data on Julian Sheldon's body. "No cranial hemorrhage, no femoral blockages, no cardiac events, nor protein strings that would indicate any kind of genetic scissoring. Ruling out all the usual sudden death suspects, I started the physical exam of the organs and found this..." he said, handing me a data sheet showing what looked to be a kidney.

I examined the image closer, zooming in on the digital reproduction that danced in front of me on the paper-thin flex screen that we called paper. "These look like crystals, Doctor".

"They are, Agent". The answer was more stern than I expected, and he raised his eyebrows at me, wide eyed anticipation awaiting my response. Dr. Corbin continued, "So, I took a sample and found that they were made of sugar. As a matter of fact,' he explained, taking a control pen and splitting the image on the data sheet in half, "these crystals go through the entire kidney. Both of them, and the bladder, actually".

"What was his blood sugar, Doctor?" I asked. "I've never seen anything like this in the field, or in any text or lesson. Kidney crystals, sure - but nothing like this!"

Dr. Corbin handed me another data card, switching the image on the sheet in my hand. "Blood sugar was zero milligrams per deciliter".

"Not possible", I came back quickly. "He'd have been dead long before is sugar got that low".

"All too true; but, nonetheless accurate. I ran the test five times. This means I have no choice but to label the death a natural one; complications from diabetes, leading to diabetic coma."

I raised my head to look at Dr. Corbin, holding the data cards and flex-sheet at my sides, staring at him in disbelief. "Diabetic coma my ass. This doesn't happen in nature, doctor. This is anything BUT natural! You can't just shuffle this away under something convenient!"

Dr. Corbin looked away, hanging his head in what I can only describe as shame. As much as I hated to see the old fellow hurting like this, I had to keep going. "Look, I know a thing or two about diabetics. Something this potentially fatal would have shown up when he was booked. Did you compare his post-mortems to the levels he had at check in?"

The doctor smiled, and lowered his voice when he responded. "Oh yes, Ms. Dyett. And the funny thing is..."

At this, the doorknob started rattling as one of the assistants fiddled for their key. Dr. Corbin look warily over his shoulder. He reached briefly in his coat pocket, then grabbed my right hand with his, placing his free hand over mine. "It seems that none of that info was gathered when the deceased was booked." As he said this, he furrowed his bushy white brow and shook his head just slightly. I felt a small push around my Quantico class ring, as something was slid beneath it. Dr. Corbin focused on my eyes as the assistant opened the door. "That being said, Agent," he said wearily, "I am afraid there is nothing more I have on the matter. I'm sorry."

****

Zim's fingers dashed across the keyboard in a hurried frenzy and I was playing lookout while he hacked into the Miami PD mainframe. Sure enough, as soon as he found the file on Julian Sheldon's intake, he could tell that data had been erased.

"See here," Zim clicked the pointer over a few screens, "and here. Large blocks of data have been overwritten with binary gibberish. It's too specific to not be intentional. Whoever did this knows this system inside and out."

"Anything you can restore from that mess, Zim?" I asked as I casually looked around the cubicle farm Zimmerman was currently calling home. Not a single person was up from their desk, or seemed to pay any attention to us, so I yawned and stretched, and turned my attention back to Zimmerman.

"Not a damn thing, Ellie. I'm good, but this

data has been overwritten at least fifty times. Even the military only does twenty-five passes before they physically destroy the platters. "

"OK, do me one last favor, then," I passed Zim the micro data card Dr. Dempsey had covertly slipped under my ring. "Pull this up and see what we have. I haven't had the time to go over it yet, but my source was too serious for this not to give us something."

While Zim started the task of decrypting the data card, Michaels buzzed me on our private comm. Forrest had given them to my team last year to field test, and we'd used them ever since for one-on-one private communication.

"Hey Ellie, can you come to security?" Michaels sounded almost too casual, adding, "There's something here you got to see."

"Be there in a few, Aaron." I responded, using the control in my pocket to end the transmission. I placed my hand on Zim's shoulder and asked, "Anything you need from me before I go?"

Zimmerman almost jumped out of his skin when I spoke, but quickly recovered and answered loudly, "No Ellie. Actually, I think I am taking the rest of the day off." With this, he reached over and yanked the power cord for his computer terminal right out of the back of the device, and in one swift motion pulled the tiny data card out of the reader and placed it almost effortlessly into his handheld unit. "Not feeling well at all. Just gonna go lay down for a bit." I immediately understood my friend and comrade, and played along. Whatever Zim was up to, I trusted him with my life; I could certainly trust him now.

"Tell you what, Shiloh," I offered, knowing that using his first name was normally a *big* no-no, but it had also become part of a private code on my team. "Why don't you go up to my flat and lay down for a bit. I'll send Aaron up in a while to take you back to your hotel."

Zim nervously replied, "Thanks, Ellie. I think I'll do that." ... then quietly added, "*and don't call me Shiloh.*"

****

I was antsy walking through the concrete corridors of the combined local and federal law enforcement offices in Miami. On some of the levels, there was a mix of FBI staff, with a few CIA and Homeland Security personnel thrown in here and there. Other levels had local police, detectives, prosecutors, and District Attorneys, all shuffling about doing their best to keep the new city safe. Then there were the shared levels; common areas that made both batches of staff feel like they were rival gangs fighting a turf war over resources, bragging rights, and the honor of calling this place "their" home, leaving the other side at the mercy of their hospitality. It was petty and childish, but it was also exactly what I had come to expect from combined local and federal offices. Add to it the fact that Zim had basically tanked our research on purpose, and I was on my guard. I knew that there had to be something big for Zimmerman to literally pull the plug, and my mind was racing across possibilities as I strode down the dimly lit hallways.

The security office was not what one would expect from a big-time building like this one. I had envisioned a large room, filled with a handful of people sitting at a few dozen monitors, and a few large screens available for special situations. The security office at Quantico was like that, as were the HQ's in New York, Boston, and San Francisco; but not here. This room might as well have been a large closet, filled with screens from floor to ceiling, and one lone operator, sitting in front of a control panel running the whole show on his own. There was barely room for me to enter when I arrived, and the low lighting, coupled with the heat of the electronics, was as bad a combination as anything I had experienced in the Dark Zone. Michaels was comfortably chatting with the security officer when I got there, and they let me in to the standing-room only space with barely a glance. For the second time today, I followed someone else's lead. Michaels had given me 'that look' when he opened the door; the one that says '*shut up and pay attention'.* So that's exactly what I did.

There are several advantages to being slight of build. For one, it makes it easier for me to hide in plain sight, and while I watched and listened to Michaels and Officer Hernandez chat about local sporting teams, movies they had seen and old girlfriends, I stayed quiet and out of the way, sliding moment by moment into a corner of the room and almost vanishing into the shadows. The monotony would be enough to make the average person drop off to sleep in this sultry, low lit room, but I had seen Michaels do this before, and I knew what he was up to. His skill in psychology was pretty amazing to me, and watching him work Hernandez into a comfort zone so quickly was as thrilling to me as watching wild animals hunt each other on the Savanna. Before he even realized it, Officer Hernandez had started giving up personal details; facts of his marriage, his personal worries - even his taxes. Aaron played the give and take game, giving just enough believable tidbits to secure the man's trust. After another ten minutes, he sprung his trap.

"So any idea what happened to the perp in block 23a last night?" Aaron asked casually. The officer squirmed a little, and surprisingly looked around the small room as though he were the one being watched.

"Hey, it's not the first time buddy. We have folks come in and never leave. Happens a lot. And I mean *a lot*; like a few a month at least."

"I haven't seen anything like that since St. Louis," Aaron offered, even though I knew it had been Zimmerman that had served in the St. Louis office. "We had so much organized crime in the Zone, we couldn't keep em all in. So our higher-ups found ways of thinning them out." Then Aaron added, "Of course, once our bosses got caught, that all stopped."

Hernandez cocked his head a little. "Really?

They got caught? Damn - that would never happen here. Too many of 'em. You better watch your butt while you guys are hanging around. I can guarantee you they are."

Hernandez turned to his console and hit a few keys, bringing up the cell block where Julian Sheldon had died. It was empty now, aside from a recovery drone using its laser to sterilize the cell. "You see these little guys? Here in Miami, they aren't just for getting rid of the dead in the zone; we use 'em to sterilize the cells people die in. Sure it serves a health purpose, but what it really does is get rid of evidence - not like any is ever left."

Then Hernandez went off on a political speech reminiscent of the Greater Depression era. He supported cleaning out the zones by force, and in his words, 'to hell with the people there'. After another few minutes of this, Hernandez' shift ended, and Michaels and his new 'friend' left the room when a new officer took over. I flashed my badge at Hernandez' replacement, stayed a few minutes to make it all look on the up and up, and left the office with more questions than I had when I had gone in.

****

Zim's handheld sat on the coffee table between scones and coffee cups, running program after program on the data card Dr. Corbin had given me. As powerful as it was, it was still far slower than using the in house computer system. After Zimmerman started spilling the beans though, I completely agreed with the slower approach.

"You'd turned to answer Michaels on the comm, and I had started running a decryption program. All of a sudden, the pointer moved on the screen by itself - just a tiny bit."

"You mean a normal person wouldn't even have noticed it?" Michaels asked, half chiding Zim's odd preoccupations with computers and half congratulating his keen observation skills.

"Exactly. That's also when I noticed that a second program was trying to access the data card. I pulled up a bypass and showed that an erasure command had been sent to the card reader. If I hadn't pulled the plug when I did, we'd have nothing here to go on. Just an empty data card."

"So someone was hacking your hack of the mainframe?" I asked, going over the data files on Julian Sheldon.

"Not exactly Ellie. That's where the problem comes in." Zim picked up his handheld and tapped a few commands, bringing up a schematic of the apartment we were in. "I brought a MR-CSA up here and scanned the room. There are, or I should say were, parallel sets of wiring going to every comm terminal, and every transmission antenna in both the rooms. I used the Crime Scene Analyzer to clip the connections, so now this room is secure." Zim passed me his other handheld, showing the diagram of the wiring in the walls, and I could see where several well-placed laser holes had cut through and severed any connections.

While I was studying the images Zim had passed to me, Michaels picked up the data pad with the holo-scan of Julian Sheldon. After a few moments, he drew a quick breath and announced, "Ellie, I think I found it."

"Found what Aaron?" I asked, turning my attention back to Michaels.

"How Julian Sheldon was murdered." With this, Michaels moved the hologram from the handheld to the overhead projector. While the detail wasn't nearly as good as the images in the holo-

84

morgue, it was good enough once enlarged to see that Sheldon had a strange bruise over his right jugular. Before I could protest, Michaels brought up Sheldon's E-MRI, and no bruise was visible.

"We can't say that means anything Aaron, and you know it. That could be post mortem for all we know."

Zim reached over and gently took the data pad from Michaels, and started tweaking the code. The enlarged image began to clear, and in the middle of the bruise, a small pinprick began to show. It looked like Sheldon had been injected with something, and the bruising had been created to cover the injection point.

After a few moments of silence, the gravity of the situation hit me. "Boys, if people are really being killed outright in the Miami Federal Building, and we've uncovered something they wanted to keep under wraps, then we could easily be their next target." Zim and Michaels nodded in agreement, both seeming to rack their brains for a solution that got us to safety while covering our tracks.

"I'll make a quick trip to the hardware store, and get the supplies to cover up the MR-CSA's handy work on the walls. At least then it won't be so obvious that we found we were being spied on."

"I'll finish my research on all this," Zim said, pulling the newly decrypted data card out of his handheld. "And just from what I can see here, there are a couple of unknown elements in Sheldon's blood work."

My boys went immediately to their tasks. While they started covering our tracks and taking apart the scaffold of lies we'd uncovered from the Miami PD, I would have to get Director Forrest involved. If it came down to it, Federal status could get us protection, but with the very walls watching us, we'd need a new place to operate sooner rather than later if we didn't plan on waking up dead the next day.

****

8
❧Anguish❧

The rest of the day was pretty uneventful. Forrest brought the girls back home from the on-site daycare around five, and they both knocked me over trying to jump in my arms when they saw me. It had been a long day for them, and for me. Chinese takeout was in order, and the girls and I ended up sitting cross-legged in the living area with Michaels, Zimmerman and Forrest all joining us for dinner. It was a simple family night, and exactly what we all needed.

I slept pretty well that night, with Erin curled up on one side, and Olivia curled up on the other. Michaels had somehow gotten Chester washed and dried, although how he managed to get the stuffed rabbit away from the girls for even five minutes was more than I could imagine. At least the girls' favorite toy no longer smelled like that nasty combination of motor oil and body odor; the gentle scent of lavender rose up from his threadbare fur.

Morning crept into the bedroom, washing the three of us in its warm sunlight. Erin only had one nightmare that night, and Olivia had no more than three. It was the best record they had since their rescue from the Dark Zone. All I could do was hope for more nights like that, and work with love and time to help them heal.

The girls were starting to pick up on my morning habits, for good or for ill. Clothes were tossed on, teeth were brushed, and we were out the door in fifteen minutes flat. Olivia even tried to comb Chester's hair, which made Erin giggle uncontrollably. I dropped them off at the daycare in the Federal Building, and headed down to the coffee shop to meet with my team to plan out the day.

My granddad always said that the biggest mistake most people make day after day is not taking the time to listen to the little voice inside them. He didn't mean the OCD voice that makes people dust their furniture fifty times a day, or the voice that tells people to wear aluminum foil under their baseball caps; he was talking about something more basic - more primal. He meant the little voice that helps you find your way when lost; the voice that tells you 'no' when you want another cookie and don't really need it. He also said we should listen to the voice that whispers dark forebodings into the corner of your ear when you run into someone you just don't trust.

When I exited the Miami Federal building, I could see Zim and Forrest waiting for me at the street corner. As I raised my arm to acknowledge them, I was nearly run over by a very large man in a black overcoat. Before I could open my mouth to apologize, he gruffly grabbed me by the arm.

"You must watch where you are going young lady. Next time, you *could* get hurt."

Under normal circumstances, I would have put his lard-laden ass on the ground as soon as he touched me, but something about this man kept me from returning the attack. I yanked my arm back and watched him continue on towards the Federal building. Forrest and Zim had seen the exchange, and were at my side before I could turn my head.

"What the hell was that, Ellie?" Forrest demanded.

I rubbed my wrist unconsciously and muttered, "Not sure. But I don't like it one bit."

I watched the obese old man turn on his heel and head into the Federal building I had just left. The voice in my head was no longer whispering; it was shouting a five alarm warning. I felt compelled to turn back and follow him in, but Zimmerman and Forrest had already started back to our coffee shop for the daily meeting we'd grown accustomed to, so I laid my granddad's advice aside and followed them, feeling like I was being the 'adult' by not giving in to a baseless fear, and going about my business. One of these days, I'll listen a little better not only to those inner voices, but to my Granddad's advice as well.

Director Forrest and I sat side by side, slowly sipping a dark French roast, and nodding while Michaels and Zimmerman gave us updates on the current situation. Michaels had gone digging for instances of other prisoners who had vanished from Miami Federal, and found missing records more often than missing people. The trail of problems was long and convoluted, and seemed to go back at least twenty years. From an outsiders standpoint, one would think that there was no way this all happened without the approval of the Facility Director, a man named Cano. If there was a cover up going on here, it was being executed by a master of the trade. No red flags had gone up since our space had been secured, so we were pretty safe for the time being.

Zim's analysis of the data card Dr. Corbin had given us was equally perplexing. No signs of sugar problems or other health issues were recorded during Sheldon's intake, but the files on the intake form in the Federal system were incomplete. One set of files was either a forgery, or had been altered in some way, but there was no visible trace that *either* file set had been tampered with. Aside from the knowledge that Julian Sheldon had to have been murdered in his cell, we had no real evidence to support the suspicion. On top of that, I really didn't care that a man who would sell his children into slavery had been killed. Harsh though it may be, I still think he got what he deserved.

After an hour or so, we all got up and headed back to our Miami office, listening to Forrest wrap up some loose ends and work on getting us back home to Mobile.

"I think we've been in Miami long enough. Maybe with Julian Sheldon out of the way, the services here can help find the girls a good home, Ellie".

What I said next surprised us all. I looked past Forrest, staring away from my team, and answered, "Yeah, but sometimes I wonder if they wouldn't be better off with me for the long run."

It had come out of my mouth before I even thought it through. Me, a single mother of two adopted twins, working the hours I work, with a sick grandfather and a world-traveling mother. How would I ever begin to entertain the thought? But there it was, just as real and solid a possibility as any I had ever considered, forcing its way past my defenses and making my real feelings known without cause or care for the repercussions.

Zim, Michaels, and Forrest stopped dead in their tracks, mouths agape at what I had just said. For what felt like hours, no one said a word. They just stood around me, my co-workers and closest friends, frozen in shock. I started to backtrack; knowing that anything I said to contradict myself would come across as disingenuous. Forrest raised his hand to stop me. I closed my mouth immediately, waiting for my boss to tap a few controls and take me off the case. It was in his power to remove the girls to a team that wouldn't be so emotionally invested in them, and our discussion a few days prior had me bracing myself for the emotional blow.

"I think that idea has merit, Ellie. Let's focus on getting things wrapped up here for now."

Director Forrest turned away, flashing me a bright smile before heading off to start his work for the day. Michaels and Zimmerman said nothing. Each patted my shoulder as they walked away, giving just enough support in the simple act of contact to assure me that they were behind me one hundred percent.

****

I couldn't go to my desk. I felt wobbly and weak, as though an inner tension I hadn't known existed had suddenly given way, and I needed a few minutes to gather myself before I could even think about the steps ahead of me. While we were guests here in Miami, I had a small cubicle instead of the small office I was accustomed to in Mobile. There is no privacy in a cubicle - so I headed to the nearest bathroom, went into the last stall, and locked the door behind me. Tears wouldn't come; nor would joy or fear, or any other logical emotion or response. For a moment I thought to myself, "*What the hell have I done?*" but the thought could barely coalesce in my head before the response came. "*What you know you wanted to do. What you need to do, for you and for them.*" I went through a roster in my mind, testing people and their likely response to my idea of adopting the girls. I quickly found that the people who mattered most to me had either already given their approval to the idea, or certainly would. The few people who were likely to reject the idea of me taking the girls were people whose opinions mattered nothing to me. "I have enough room already. Mom will just have to use a hide-a-bed when she comes to visit."

I sat there on the commode, door shut, listening to my thoughts and the echo of others as they came and went. After ten minutes, I stood, wiping away a single tear that had slowly built up in my right eye, and opened the stall door. People were coming and going, life went on, and I might end up having two little girls. A wide grin materialized on my face, with a feeling behind it so profound that I couldn't have stopped it even if I had wanted to.

I moved toward the restroom exit, but my way out, I overheard two women talking at the sinks.

"He was just so rough," said one woman, as she leaned over the basin and applied her lipstick.

"Abrasive, eh?" her friend replied. "I kinda like 'em that way."

The first woman shook her head, "Not this one. He had to be four hundred pounds at least."

At this I stopped, a sense of foreboding welling up in my throat. Granddaddy used to say we all had a little monster inside us, hopefully trapped in a cage in the back of our minds. The little beast in the back of my head was screaming loudly, crying in anguish with the fear of what was to come.

The woman continued, "And that black coat was filthy. You'd almost think he lived in the Zone."

I was now paralyzed in fear, unable to think or feel or react. I had to hear the rest. The woman, who was slim and likely in her early forties, finally finished applying her lipstick. Her next words cut into me with a searing pain.

"I swear if all his credentials hadn't checked out, I never could have let those little girls go with him".

****

"I promise it all checked out!" Agent Gallindo proclaimed as he pulled up all the data card scans he'd gotten when releasing the girls not an hour before. "Look, right here," he said, pulling up the holographic image and throwing it in the air between us all for review. The woman from the bathroom was sitting in the corner shaking, mascara running down her face and a balled up handkerchief in her still trembling hand. Gallindo continued, bringing up more scans of ID's and birth records.

"Here you go; Michael E. Carter, 1626 Estebaren Way, Miami. Born July 2nd, 2022. Birth records show it was a multiple birth, with Madeline Francis Carter, who we know is the birth mother of Erin and Olivia Carter."

I couldn't open my mouth. When I heard the girls were gone, I had a minor breakdown. Zimmerman told me later that he heard me three floors up, and that there wasn't anything 'minor' about it; it was a wailing so sorrowful that agents in the building reported its sound had stopped everyone who heard it. It was a mournful sound so intense that hearing it drift through the halls of the Federal Building caused some to think the end of the world was upon them. I had cried so hard, screamed so long, that for the moment I had no voice. All I could do was sit and listen, and suppress the urge to rip Gallindo's spleen out through his nostrils.

Forrest stepped in, barely concealing his anger. "You were the Assistant Director in Charge at the time, Gallindo. And you couldn't be bothered to call us? Is this how you people work in Miami?"

Gallindo looked sheepish, shuffling through more data rather than look Forrest or me in the eyes. "Local policy, sir. We have had so many illegals over the years, it just became too time consuming to do a full background check on someone if they already had proper paperwork. Michael Carter HAD all the proper paperwork! My hands were tied."

Zimmerman had grabbed the holographic image of the scanned Identification, and been working on determining its authenticity. He shook his head angrily, almost shouting at Gallindo. "It's not a lot of work to see this is a fake, you lazy son of a ..."

Forrest interrupted him, placing a hand between Gallindo and Zim. "Hold on, Zimmerman. We're all angry and hurt here, but we either work together on this or we find out nothing." I could see Forrest was barely in control of his own emotions, but the fact that he could keep Zim and Gallindo from having a fist-fight showed me once again why he was our boss. It was in his blood to keep his cool and seek out the facts; kicking ass was a last resort for Forrest, no matter how upset or hurt he was.

Forrest took a moment to let Zim cool down, then asked, "Will you show me what you found?"

Zim reached over and manipulated the holoscan of the ID to enlarge it sixteen hundred times. He pointed to a small, thin line in the pixels. "Right here, sir. This line shouldn't be here. It's a cut and paste job if I have ever seen one."

A look of realization crept onto Gallindo's face. "Mr. Zimmerman," he asked quietly. "Would you mind taking a look at this birth record please?"

Zim took the hologram and started cross-referencing the information. It took him less than ten seconds before he spoke. "I had already pulled all the pertinent info on the girls' mother, Madeline F. Carter. According to her records, hers was a single birth. She has no twin brother."

Gallindo sat down hard, almost missing the chair. I looked at him and managed to whisper, "Now you know how I feel."

Zim continued, "Hold on - looks like the photo for Michael Carter matches an IAFIS entry for a Prospero Pizzano." Zim tapped a few controls on his handheld and continued, "and he has a similar record to Julian Sheldon. Looks like they were in Juvenile detention together..." Zim hit a few more keys, "and jointly owned a shipping company set up close to the Zone and to Pier 23."

Zim pulled up the photo I had snapped in the holo-recreator, and soon made a match. "Looks like that shipping company is in the same zip code as the address that Grummold had for the girls."

The news made me feel more sick than I had earlier. I was drowning in an emotional riptide that I wasn't strong enough to free myself from, and every new bit of information pulled me under more and more. The screams were gone, as were the tears. I sat in shock, with anger eating me up from the inside, and a heart so broken that I couldn't think about whether I lived or died. My girls were not only gone, but had been taken right from under our noses by a companion of the man who tried to sell them into a hellish existence.

Michaels opened the meeting room door so forcefully that the floating holograms rippled in his wake. Sweat poured from his brow, and he shut the door and nearly collapsed in the last free space.

"I couldn't find him. I followed the taxi from the surveillance footage for at least two miles, but they're just... gone."

"So that's it," I whispered. "They're gone."

Michaels sat up and pulled Gallindo close to him, forcing the man to look him in the face. "Well, that depends on you, Sparky. Tell me, when you were letting them go, did the girls have their toy rabbit with them?"

Gallindo's eyes were wide and confused. "Their what? What are you talking about? Does it matter?"

Michaels stood to his full six-foot-six-inch height, lifting Gallindo with him, and picked him up by the collar to look him straight in the eyes once more. "The white rabbit." he said, in an eerily calm, quiet voice. "Did they have him when they left?"

Gallindo's eyes darted from side to side. After a moment, he said "Yes. Yes, I'm sure they did!"

"Then we can find them." With this, Michaels dropped Gallindo and sat back down, bringing out his own handheld computer and pulling up a map. He hit some controls, and the map focus changed to show an outline of New Miami, with a glowing red dot just coming to a stop. He shifted the vantage again to a side view, and the dot moved to show it was not in New Miami - it was under it, in the Dark Zone below.

"I figured the girls would be with us for a long time Ellie, so when I washed and dried Chester the other day, I put a transponder inside him. As long as their rabbit is with them, we know where they are."

The dark oppression in my mind suddenly felt lifted, and the full force of anger within me nearly threw me out of my seat. Furrowing my brow, I looked at the map and the red dot that showed me where my girls were being held.

"Then we go get them," I whispered to my boys. "We go in, and we bring them home."

9
❧Stasis❧

Have you ever seen a hungry lioness tempted with raw meat? It's not a pretty sight; given only water, the lioness will become more and more aggressive over a period of hours. If this torture is continued over a few days, the lioness is understandably driven to a point of near insanity, where she will take any risk to get to the flesh dangled before her.

It was a given that I would go get my girls. Like the aforementioned lioness, it would have been impossible to keep me away, regardless of the risk. That being said, bureaucratic bull crap was keeping me from acting, pushing my anger well beyond its boiling point, and driving me into a frenzy that was dangerous for me, my team, and my girls. Three days had passed since Prospero Pizzano had walked right into Miami Federal, presented fake credentials and walked out with two rescued children. There was already a buzz in the underworld of a new auction, and I had no doubt in my mind that Erin and Olivia were in more danger now than they had ever been.

Michaels and Zim created a program to alert me when the tracker in the girls' toy rabbit made the slightest move. They had been shuffled around several times the first day, and had barely moved an inch since then. I was happy for any movement, because it told me that Chester hadn't been tossed in a rubbish bin. As long as he was allowed to stay with the girls, as long as he moved even a little, I could hold my anger at bay and spend my time making plans. Of course it was possible that Chester had been discarded, but I couldn't consider that possibility. The old stuffed rabbit was my only link to my girls, and I couldn't let my hope become as threadbare as he was. It was all that was keeping me from a complete shutdown.

****

Thursday was not shaping up to be a good day. I arrived in my cubicle to find no less than seven emails from different team leads in the area, all of whom had pledged their assistance the day before, and were revoking that pledge this morning. I clicked thru each communication, feeling the small walls of the cubicle close in on me, and a deep rage building inside me. The last email was from Director Forrest; it had no subject. The body of the communication said only "Coffee Shop".

At this point coffee was the last thing I needed. I was so angry, shaking so badly, that I could hardly log out of the computer terminal. No one spoke to me on my way out; hell, they barely looked at me, as though the very act of noticing me would incur my vengeance. Considering the emotional turmoil I had been going through, they were probably right. After all, a hungry lioness is bad, but a hungry lioness in a cage is far worse.

The coffee shop was crowded for a Thursday morning, and it took me a few minutes to find Director Forrest, sitting with Michaels and Zimmerman in the back corner at a much smaller table than we were used to. I approached the table, but before I could ask what the hell was going on, Forrest motioned for me to sit, and Zim pulled out a chair for me.

"Ellie, there's no easy way to say this." Jim began, fiddling with his coffee cup, but not daring to bring it up to his lips. "Washington has closed the

Miami Dark Zone. We have, for the foreseeable future, no way in or out."

"What?!" I exclaimed, suppressing the urge to jump out of my seat and scream. "Why?"

Forrest now took a brief sip from his coffee, then took a deep breath before he answered. "Seems that something is brewing in the Miami Zone. Recon shows an almost military level buildup down there. Director Cano has reported that they've managed to bring in weapons that have been outlawed since the Twenty-teens, and they've brought in enough fire power to besiege a city. The FBI is out-manned and outgunned, and Washington doesn't want to provoke them."

"And?" I answered, trying not to sound too arrogant. "Michaels and I can get in, grab the girls, and get out. No army needed. Hell, I was wondering if a smaller operation might not be better anyway."

"No, Ellie. I want them out and safe as much as you do, but we have been locked down. We're not currently allowed in - period."

The caged, starving lioness within me was barely controlling her urge to pounce. I started to open my mouth, but Forrest raised a hand and continued, leaning closer to me, and signaling Michaels and Zimmerman to do the same.

"Ellie, I asked to meet you here to tell you this for two reasons. One, you were more likely to behave if you were in a crowded public place. Two, it gives me the opportunity to do this." Forrest leaned in more, getting close enough for me to smell his subtle after shave. His lips came close to my ear, and he whispered, barely audible, "You find a way in, and I'll cover you." He then sat back, finished his coffee, and said aloud, "I'm sorry Ellyandra. There isn't anything else I can do about it."

Michaels and Zimmerman stayed at the table with me, not bothering to ask what had been said in confidence. I was sure they already knew. I was also sure that Jim was taking a big chance. He didn't want me in a position to disobey a direct order, but he couldn't let the girls go any easier than I could. I sat at the table, ignoring the cruller and java that my boys had placed in front of me, turning over scenario after scenario, trying to find something that could not only be believable, but could be executed quickly.

After forty minutes of contemplation, I finally found what I was looking for. It was hidden in the creases of my memory; it was one of the many sharp edges in my brain that I always seemed to find when a particular someone came to mind. It was a memory so small and seemingly unlikely that it almost bordered on a memory from a dream. Did it really happen or not? Not knowing had brought me to my knees in the past, and even though I had long come to terms with it, the inconclusiveness of the memory still made my stomach sink. The fact that it came to mind now, while I was trying to find a way to rescue my girls, proved to me that I already loved them more than I loved anyone or anything else.

"Zim, I need your help." I leaned over, and my boys did the same as I whispered, "Can you get me a secure line? There is someone I need to talk to."

****

Zim, Michaels, and I sat on the rooftop of the Miami Federal building. Seventy-three floors up, the wind was so strong here that we almost needed safety lines to keep from blowing over.

"Why are we here, Shiloh?' Michaels asked Zimmerman. Zim's face started turning red and he spat out, "Damnit, don't call me Shiloh!" Zim tweaked a few wires from one of the dozen or so antenna arrays on the rooftop, and hooked them into one of his secured handheld units. "Look, I bypassed security protocols on transmissions by hitting the source right at the array junction. Basically, our transmission will look like static to anyone else, and it won't be able to be decrypted, because that's happening on a secondary system." He raised his handheld, tapping it slightly on the side.

"Where is he then, Zim?' I asked as he brought the system up.

Zimmerman scanned a US Map for almost six minutes before responding, "Colorado Springs, Ellie. Looks like he is speaking at a symposium today."

"Patch me thru, Zim. I don't care what he's doing, just get me through."

Charles McFarland stood at his podium, looking out on a lecture hall filled with some of the best and brightest minds of the decade. He'd had big moments before, but his research had never again reached the level of excitement and fulfillment as it had when he was 24, and discovered a way to regenerate optic nerve fibers. It had made him wealthy within a year, and brought him 'fame and glory'. Then had come the inevitable 'what's next' questions, and life took a turn on him. Research funds would no longer be an issue - he was set for life now. Sadly, accomplishments were suddenly few and far between, and nothing he had done had even come close to changing the human condition in the way that curing blindness had done. He'd peaked at 24, and been struggling ever since. No matter how wealthy, successful, or how renowned, Charles McFarlane kept struggling to overcome the successes of his early life. Now, he was about to speak in front of his colleagues for the first time in almost three years, presenting new research on the chemical induction of Psychosis. Charles looked out on the growing crowd, then back to his notes on the paper-like electronic screen before him.

A sick feeling washed over him as the screen went fuzzy, almost like old analog television static. Then his notes - his treasured research, started to move around on the page, each letter contorting and adjoining until they all came together to form a face. It was the face of his friend and former fiancée, Ellyandra Dyett.

Words started typing themselves out on the page. "Charles, I know you can't hear me. There is an emergency, and I need you like I have never needed you before." Even in black and white, he could almost see the vibrant red curls bouncing around her face, and almost hear her voice. "*Damnit Ellie, why now?* " He wasn't sure how, but she could apparently see him, because she responded "Because if I wait, even a little while, two children will be dead in the worst kind of way. I need your help Charlie. Please."

The lights in the room began to dim as the crowd settled down for his lecture. Charles looked out on the crowd - his future - then looked back to the page - the face of his past. She was the biggest reminder of his successes and his failures, and even though she would always be his friend, she was also still a reminder of the choice he had made.

He knew her in ways no one else could, and she knew him in ways he wished she didn't. Still, it was unlike Ellie to come right out and ask for help. She'd toy with him, coerce him, and even blackmail him if needed; but to just cut to the chase and ask was new.

With a 'damn' muttered under his breath, Charles looked out to the crowd and announced, "Ladies and Gentlemen, I know it's bad timing, but the equipment is having some technical glitches that just presented themselves. Please help yourselves to more coffee and pastries, and allow me thirty minutes to get this resolved. Thank you."

****

"You need what!?" Charles shouted once he and I had a secured line in a more private space. "You mean to tell me that I am out here trying to restart my career and change the direction of Psychological Medicine, and you HACK YOUR WAY into my panel to have me help you hitch a ride into the Miami Dark Zone? What the hell are you thinking Ellie?"

"Charles, there are two kidnapped girls in there, and HQ has shut out all access. I have no legitimate way in, and the full force of hell isn't keeping me from going to get them. Now I know you and your 'work' Charlie," I paused, trying not to let my anger get away with me. "I know that your current research comes from the situation you helped me with last year, but I know some of your other 'sources' could get your ass thrown under the jail. Do NOT make me threaten you Charles!"

Charles thought quietly for a moment, the redness in his cheeks diffusing slightly. "So, if I get you in, there are no questions, right?" Before I could answer, he continued, "Because quite frankly there

111

are some of these folks that would rather *not* know what all they are up to. My dealings with them are quick and simple, and whatever else they do I do not want to know about. Understand, Ellie?"

"I believe you. Please Charles, just do whatever you need to do to get me in there."

10
❧Subterfuge❧

Charles was true to his word. In an hour's time, we had received encoded communications on where we would meet a boat that scooted us a hundred miles out to sea. The boat was a small fishing vessel that was either unaccustomed to having visitors or designed to look that way. The old sea dog that piloted the ship said barely two words to us, staring out at the horizon with its shades of blue and grey with flashes of red, violet, and yellow. The days were long this time of year, and it felt like forever before night finally took us.

Michaels and I stood next to the railing, watching the sky darken, and become one with the sea. Aside from the bobbing up and down of the waves, we could have been floating in space after the sun set. The boat wasn't running any light, and we drifted in silence, waiting for what was to come. Michaels and I already had a plan, but until we actually got into the zone and assessed the situation, we had no way of knowing how useful that plan would be.

At least thirty minutes passed (or was it two hours - impossible to tell) before we knew our passage into the Miami zone had arrived. It started with a bubbling from beneath the ship; that quickly built into wave after wave shooting up around us, then the boat being physically lifted out of the water as a massive submarine surfaced beneath us. The sub had a platform or sorts built into its frame, and out little schooner easily fit into the V-shaped niche that was obviously designed to capture ships in one fell swoop. No sooner than Michaels and I had found our footing, a large metal turret extended from the top of the sub, right next to the platform that held our boat. A walking plank extended from beneath the doorway which opened, revealing light that seemed so bright to our eyes as to blind us. A dark silhouette emerged from the doorway, square shoulders emphasized by old style naval trapping from decades long gone. Behind this man came two others, carrying a chest between them. They quickly deposited the chest in front of the old captain who'd brought us this far, then retreated back into the light.

As the silhouettes' features began to grow from the shadows, he spoke, with a thick Slavic accent. "Welcome aboard the *MURDERER'S SLAVE*. You will do as you are told, speak when spoken to, and touch nothing, or I will feed you to the sharks." His tone never lifted in anger; it wasn't a threat, just a statement of fact. We were just slightly above captives in his book, and aside from our eventual freedom, we had no expectation of rights on his ship. He continued, "If this is understood, then please, come aboard." His tone was almost genteel as he bowed slightly and waved his arm across, stepping aside for Michaels and I to pass. I grabbed my gear and strapped it down to the black armourweave Michaels and I had both outfitted ourselves in, and covertly made sure my hidden comm was active. Just because Charles McFarlane was using these criminals to get us into the Zone didn't mean he trusted them, and I wasn't about to throw away the only lifeline I had to the outside while in their 'care'.

We were lead not to a holding room, but to the bridge, and instructed in grunts and shoves to a pair of seats next to the captain's position. As he sat, the engineers and pilots worked to submerge the vessel, and we could hear the creaks and groans not only of the schooner leaving its impromptu dry-dock above us, but the sound of the water increasing its pressure on the hull. The bridge almost looked like a movie set, but it didn't take me long to realize that we were in an old Soviet era nuclear Submarine. I had seen pictures of the bridge of the Kursk when the wreck was raised, and aside from more modern, upgraded electronics, the structure was the same. The creaking of the hull finally leveled out, and the Captain, who had not given us his name, quietly said "Dopredu pln'y". It was either Russian, or some variant of, but I could feel the submarine pick up forward momentum. Michaels and I looked at each other, not saying a word lest we incur the wrath of the Captain and his crew, and waited.

****

I had a friend in College that used to tell me about getting in trouble for falling asleep in the car on short trips. She went through a phase in her teens that drove her parents nearly crazy, when she would sit and stare at them instead of converse or work together to solve problems. From what I was told, the real issue wasn't that she would fall asleep, but that she refused to try anything that her family offered to help her stay awake. Her mom and dad died while we were in College, and now Sarah remembered those times sheepishly with regret. Still, despite the ghost of teenage drama that came with the memory, there were times that I would catch myself nodding when I really wasn't supposed to, and the thought of this story would bring me back to consciousness with a jolt.

This time, the jolt didn't come from my memory, it came from above. We suddenly decelerated, and I had to reach out and grab Michaels to keep from hitting the floor with a thud. A warning claxon was sounding, and some of the older electronics were blinking in and out of functionality. The Captain was half standing from his command, perched at the edge barking orders that I couldn't understand. From a nearby speaker, I could hear a transmission.

"This is the USS Gallatim. You have left international waters and punctured the southeastern perimeter of the United States Secure Zone. By Order of, and with the Authority of Homeland Security, you are hereby commanded to surface for boarding, or we will sink you. You have two minutes to comply."

The captain and crew started in a frenzy, angling the nose of the craft for a steep dive. In all the hubbub, I could hear Zim in my earpiece. "Ellie?

Ellie - are you there? Naval intercept shows a submarine has been spotted on what I assume would be your course. Are you safe?"

I knew I was taking a chance by answering, but I softly whispered, "No Zim. Not at all. Gallatim has us. Thoughts?"

The captain took note of my voice, but did not act. He apparently had the hearing of a rabbit to have even noticed me in all the ambient noise, but he was spending his time forging a getaway.

Zim chimed in. "I'm connected to Gallatim's systems Ellie. They are getting ready to attack, and they can see your trajectory. If you dive lower now, you will head right into a dozen depth charges.

I jumped up quickly, and grabbed the Captain by the arm. His soldiers immediately leveled firearms at me, but I held on as he struggled, shouting at him, "Don't dive! It's a trap!"

It took three men to pull me off him, but they hadn't shot me yet. Michaels had been restrained as soon as I leapt on the captain, so he couldn't help me. The Captain gave the order of "Robinzonada! Robinzonada!", immediately followed by "Spustenie navnad a povrch! Teraz!" The ship fired empty missile shells down along its trajectory, then creaked and cried out as the angle changed from a dive to a sharp surfacing. Water sprayed out of pipes overhead and the pressure change felt like it would make my head explode. The ship broke the surface of the water, almost leaping out like a charging whale, within a few feet of the Gallatim. The immense displacement of water caused the surface ship to nearly capsize, and our Captain took the upper hand, grabbing what looked like a joystick from an old video game, and targeting the Coast Guard Cutter. Before I could protest, he had already aimed and fired, sending an electromagnetic pulse at the ship that shut it down almost instantly. The Gallatim now bobbed on the surface like a useless bottle, and we slid smoothly back under the waves.

****

We didn't surface again for twenty minutes, and each of those minutes was spent with guns aimed straight at our heads. When Michaels and I were finally lead topside, the door in the turret slid aside to reveal open water right at our feet. First I was thrown off into the cold water of Miami's zone, with Michaels right behind me. I treaded water to look back at the Captain and said, "You know I saved your ass!"

As he closed the door behind him, he answered, "I know. That is why I am throwing you into water that has no sharks."

The black metal turret of the submarine slipped quietly away from us, diving as it departed, and leaving Michaels and I with half a miles' swim to the waterfront of the Zone. Now the real work would begin.

11
❧Inveiglement❧

The swim into the zone was probably the nastiest thing I had ever experienced. The garbage that I could see ranged from floating bins of hospital sharps to used sanitary napkins and dead animals. Even in the dark, the lights from the city ahead reflected just enough to let us know that we didn't really want to know what other kind of sludge we were swimming in. I was more and more grateful for having no cuts or bruises, and for being up to date on all my immunizations, because God only knows what I would have caught had that not been the case.

As we got closer to the Zone, a faint glow could occasionally be seen from below the new city. Once we finally climbed up the wreckage of Pier 23 and made it ashore, I could see what was causing the glow. Ahead, large spotlights were being installed on some of the buildings. They were all being pointed inward. Michaels took out his binoculars, and used the digital enhancement to take a better look.

"Looks like they've drilled right up through the city platforms above and tapped directly into the power grid. So now they will have power and light."

"And more weapons," I added, showing Michaels a crate of Automatics I had uncovered while he surveyed the work above. "No wonder HQ locked out the Zone. We're in deep here, Aaron. We need to find the girls and get out."

We crouched behind the warehouse closest to Pier 23, where the girls and I had snuck through during our first escape. It was quiet now, at least on the outside. Lights were on inside, and the noise that hid our presence also told me that it was far from quiet inside. But right then, at that moment, I couldn't care less what they were doing in there. I was here for two things - Erin and Olivia. The rest of the Miami Zone could burn for all I cared, as long as I could bring my girls out in one piece.

Michaels had to work for several long minutes to get the tracking device to power up; the swim hadn't been great for any of our gear. Most of it was waterproof to some degree, but even waterproof equipment had a difficult time being submerged in the nastiness we had come through. Michaels handed the device to me, pointing out the small red blip on the display. I looked over the map on the small screen and compared it to the map in my memory from almost a month's stay in this place.

"There is no way we are getting there un-noticed dressed like this. Too many populated areas to cross through." I kept reviewing the map with the blinking red dot that told me where my girls were, then showed it to Michaels, pointing out, "We're here. They're there... and if we can make it to here," I said, shoving a finger two blocks north west of our current position, "then I have a plan."

One thing I had learned quickly was if you were going to live in the Zone, you were either prepared to risk the streets, or you found a place - any place - you could call home. I had been on recon for two days before I found the Valencia and made it my home-away-from-home. Its orange painted concrete facade was lined with dozens of storm proof windows that had amazingly gone unbroken since its abandonment. Back in the day, the old building had been part of a six-story office park, but once it was buried in the Zone, it became a home for the homeless, a crack den for the drug addled, and a resource for people like Grummold, who used all the free space to build a small criminal empire. While the other buildings close by had fallen in on themselves, the Valencia still stood, almost fort-like in the shadows of the Dark Zone.

We were lucky that the spotlights being installed around the Zone were trained toward its center. That gave us enough shadow to work our way covertly around the blocks and over to the building that I had called home for my month-long stint here in purgatory. There were more people out and about in the Zone now than there had been before, and every one we saw was armed to the teeth. Michaels and I had to stay hidden, jumping and running from shadow to shadow, trying to avoid being seen by any of the men or women wandering around like prison guards. Finally, after an hour of carefully placed steps and more near-misses than I care to count, we made it inside the Valencia.

The old building had been practically falling down when I was here before, but I could tell from the entryway that something had changed. Gone was the litter and boxes of trash I had walked passed daily. The place was far from clean, but it was no longer ruinous either. Also missing were the dozens of drug-addled men, women and teens that had come in and found a place to sit and enjoy their trip. The place was empty - completely empty. When I was here before, each stairwell had been filled with people in a drug-induced fog, who were never even aware that I was stepping over them. Now, the steps had been swept clean. The dance I had made around them for almost a month was no longer needed, and Michaels and I walked straight up the stairwell of the empty building to level five, through the empty hallway, and down to the last office on the corner.

The glare of the spotlights outside bounced through the outer windows and around the otherwise darkened corridor, making superbrights or nightvision goggles useless. Someone could have easily hidden not five feet away from me in the darkness, and I'd never have known they were there. The door to my little 'apartment' was slightly ajar, so I cautiously opened it and went inside, Pulser drawn, ready to strike down anything or anyone that chose to jump from the ever-shifting shadows.

Inside things were exactly as I had left them. I approached an old filing cabinet had served as a dresser, and reached inside to pull out raggedy clothes for Michaels and me to wear over our armourweave. They smelled putrid, and were dirty and nasty, but they were still far better than the sewage we had swum through on the waterfront.

Michaels looked around a bit, exploring the small kitchenette with a non-working sink and moldy fridge, then making his way around a pile of broken desks and chairs to find the tiny pallet of blankets I had called a bed. "You really lived here, didn't you?" he asked. I nodded as I approached him with the clothes to disguise himself. "Why did you choose here, Ellie?"

He took the clothes from me as I answered. "It was a simple choice; the door actually locked. That one asset made this place more safe for me than any other place I found in the Zone."

As I said this, I looked over to the door that had kept out the wandering junkies while I had been here, and noticed something new. Just above the

126

doorframe was a small, blinking red light. It sat within an inch of the molding, almost out of sight, but there it was. I could guarantee that it had not been here during my stay in the Zone, and I immediately gave Aaron the 'Shut up" sign.

Aaron nodded, and we both made a quick sweep of the office, making sure we were alone. I slowly crept up along the wall, trying to stay out of sight of the red light. It could have been anything; a motion sensor, a scanner, a microphone - you name it. And until I found out what it was, I wasn't taking any chances.

I finally reached the door that had locked behind us, and when I touched the handle, I received a high power shock that almost threw me across the room. The blinking red light was now glowing steady, and a quiet little *beep* rang in the air. First, it rang out, each beep a second apart, but then the pace picked up, getting faster and higher pitched. A voice erupted from the back of the room, and Aaron and I turned our Pulsers on the bluish, glowing figure of Grummold. I couldn't tell where the hologram was being projected from, and as the red light above the door grew faster and brighter, the hologram spoke.

"You see, little girl, I have my ways of

finding things out, and I had a feeling you'd come back here. So, here is a little something to satiate my need for vengeance!" The hologram pointed at the light, which was now emitting heat and a sound so high pitched, it felt like my ears were going to start bleeding. The hologram of Grummold now stood, laughing at us, waiting for us to die. Whether or not it was a live feed didn't matter - he might as well have been right there, telling me I couldn't have my girls back.

The sound and heat were getting to us, making Michaels and I weak and tired. I looked over to him, and we nodded at each other, gathering our strength and standing in unison. Aaron and I leveled our Pulsers at the door and pulled the triggers, blowing it off its hinges, and allowing us to tear out of the room and down the hall, just barely reaching the concrete stairwell before a firebomb erupted behind us.

We didn't bother to look back; we took the rear exit of the building, ran around the corner, then worked our way back, trying hard to blend in as fast as possible with the growing crowd. It wasn't long before the fire burned itself out, and the crowd dispersed enough for us to leave without drawing any special attention to ourselves. Michaels and I walked off, and found some space behind a few dozen piled up crates so we could check the tracker. The girls' position had not waivered, and for the first time in the days since they had been taken, I found no comfort in that small fact. Grummold had laid a trap for me, and I had sprung it. He knew I was coming.

12
❧Incursion❧

I remember running barefoot at my Nana's house as a little girl. She died when I was five, and had been the only connection I ever had with my father. I guess my most vivid memory of her revolves around ants. Strange, I know, but still, anytime I see ants swarming, I think of Nana. One time, while running through her yard, trying hard to get up enough momentum to fly, I ran right through an anthill. Not fire-ants, but still one of those 'southern' anthills that rival those in the Amazonian rainforest. Nana saw me fall, and like any good grandmother, came running to check on me. In the twenty seconds or so that it took her to reach me, the angry black ants I had inadvertently made homeless had enveloped both my legs, each of the little buggers biting over and over again. Nana came to the rescue, using her own bare hands to sweep the biting critters off my exposed fragile skin. Two hours and a trip to the emergency room later, my legs and her hands were both covered in bandages that dripped with foul-smelling ointments. So many of my memories of her are out of focus, like dreams, or events that happen when you are feverish; the line between what you remember and what really was is a fuzzy one at best. Still, I will never forget the look on her face as she swept the ants off me. In that memory, her face is more crisp and clear than any portrait, and she is more real to me than in any other recollection.

Walking the streets of the zone now made me think of Nana. The streets had been crowded before, but after Michaels and I escaped the firebomb that had been left for us, people swarmed like ants all around us. Hundreds, if not thousands of drunk, drug addicted, sick, deranged and very well-armed miscreants were crawling the streets, up and over abandoned cars and empty crates, even scrambling up the sides of buildings to the old fire escapes. We were being pulled along in a sea of angry, violent people, and part of me wished that my Nana would come, her kind face smiling at me, and sweep all these people away.

I took Michaels by the hand, and together, we worked our way through the tide of bodies toward one of the alleyways nearby. All around, people were tossing off their nightvision goggles as the newly installed spotlights were pointed upward, casting a bright spot on the concrete ceiling above, and reflecting illumination down like an artificial sun. There were still shadows for us to hide in, but those shadows were a dwindling resource that we could no longer count on.

"El, we have got to get to the girls." Michaels said, his voice almost lost in the excitement of the still-growing crowd. "We need to figure out exactly where we are."

I nodded, reaching into my pocket and hitting the tiny remote control for the comm unit in my ear. It sat in my ear canal almost like an old-style hearing aid, and took its power from the heat generated by my body. Watertight and essentially glued in place with a protein based epoxy, these mini-comms were our lifelines between each other. I had grown so accustomed to it that I often forget it was there.

"Zim, you there?" I asked to the wind.

"Ellie! We were getting worried!" Zim's panic

was evident as he rambled out more questions. " Where are you? Did you make it into the Zone? What's going on?"

"No time for details Zim. Can you locate us? "

I could hear clicking on the keyboard as Zim searched his resources.

"Nope. Even using the comm-link as a tracer, my results are inconclusive. I'll keep trying to tap into the old street camera system, but that seems down at the moment."

Michaels used my body as a shield between the crowd and the building we'd reached, checking the tracking unit as covertly as possible. "Two blocks north-northeast. If these alleys are passable, we can be there in twenty minutes tops."

Michaels had turned his comm on as well, so Zimmerman could follow us by voice if nothing else. We worked our way through the alleyway closest to us, and out onto another street that was quickly filling with what looked like a poorly organized militia. You could see people hoisting everything from anti-aircraft weapons to rifles and RPG launchers, too many of them wild-eyed with an unhealthy exuberance that made them all the more dangerous. We ended up taking a few streets here, going out of our way there, and finally after what seemed like hours, reached the building we were looking for. The worst of the crowds had thinned out enough for Michaels to check the tracker without having to hide behind me. According to the now-steady red light on the tracking device, my girls were three floors up, and closer to me than they had been in days.

The old building looked more like hell in the faux sunlight of the Zone than it had in nightvision. Apparently surfaced scorched at some point in the past, the brick facade looked to be barely holding up, and in several places, you could see where the walls had been shorn up with makeshift steel I-beams, concrete blocks, and any other material they had been able to get their hands on. To be as run-down as it was, it was very well guarded. No less than sixteen men walked a perimeter around the place, each dressed like soldiers in a private little army. The difference between these men and the overly-armed crowds we'd seen was obvious. The crowd was an informal militia; these men were professionals.

One of the spotlights across the zone from us suddenly failed, plunging us into a twilight of sorts. The lights on our side of the zone were still working, but they were pointed basically away from our position. It wasn't dark, but we now had a little more cover to work with, and I planned to use it. Looking around, I found that the building across the street was not guarded at all. I tapped Michaels on the hand, using signals to show him where I wanted to go, and soon we broke into the lower entrance and stepped down into a sunken room. Mold and mildew filled the air, telling me we were either close to the water level, or this place had never dried out after the last major hurricane flooded the zone. Michaels and I took out micro-fiber breathing masks to keep ourselves from succumbing to the potentially deadly mold bloom, and quickly found the way out and up, carefully testing each step of the wooden floors to make sure we wouldn't fall through. Another half hour passed before we found a safe path up to the third floor, and reached a window that faced the building where my girls were being held. I took the scanning binoculars from Michaels, and looked across to the well-guarded building, looking in each window for any signs of Erin or Olivia. Wherever they were, they weren't visible from a window.

"Got the dragonfly, Aaron?" I asked, still whispering. Michaels answered with a small grunt in the affirmative. "OK, Let's tap her into the binoculars, and see what we can see."

135

Michaels took a small plastic case out of one of the many pouches strapped to the armourweave beneath his clothes, and placed it on the tracking device. He hit a small button on the side, opening the case and revealing what looked like a small, metal dragonfly. The tracking device immediately noticed, and with unseen transmissions and computer protocols that only Zimmerman could understand, the tracker display shifted and reorganized into a remote control for the tiny flying recon bug. Michaels tapped a few more controls, and the view in my binoculars changed from the view of the lenses to the eyes of the dragonfly. I now saw what it saw, but I had all the added features of the scanning binoculars as well.

Even if we had been in broad daylight, with systems knowing where to look, the dragonfly would have been missed by almost anything. Here in the dusk-like light of the Miami Zone, the dragonfly cruised completely unnoticed over the heads of the guards below. Looking through the binoculars, I felt like I was flying, over and around, and into an open window. I was in. The rooms swam around as the dragonfly darted and danced in the air currents, going from room to room, looking down from very near the ceiling, surveying each space for my girls. It wasn't long before I found them, not stuck in a cage as they had been before, but lying on the dirty floor, their new clothes marred with filth, hands tied together with binding wire, and each unconscious. Olivia had peed herself at some point, and the dark stain of the event spread out on her clothes and the floor beneath her. Erin was propped up against the wall, eyes rolled back in her head. While Olivia looked like a small corpse, Erin was obviously drugged. God only knows what they had been given to make sure they didn't try and run away, and a sick anger started to take me. Many times in my life, I had been so angry I cried. Mama Jerri used to tell me that if you saw tears in her eyes, and no one was dead, just wait, because she was probably mad enough to kill someone. My mother was the same way, and until that moment I had been too. But this was a different kind of anger, unlike anything I had felt before. I stood up, tossed Michaels the binoculars, and went to the corner of the room, throwing up all the way.

It was several minutes before I could tell Aaron what I had seen. He didn't throw up, but his disdain for the men who had the girls was evident. Now that we knew where they were in the building, we just needed to find a way in, and while part of me wanted the head-on confrontation of going in and kicking ass, I knew that would more than likely lead to my being shot in the head, and my girls being left to be sold. This called for sneakiness, planning, and no small degree of mischief, and as Michaels and I made our way back out of the dilapidated structure, noise from one street away gave me an idea.

13
❧Distraction❧

I soon knew why the noise one street over from where my girls were being held was so intense. This was the street where weapons were being passed out. More armed professionals were here, protecting crate after crate of gear, and controlling the bloodthirsty crowd as each of the people were given their arms.

"Swords to Plowshares, isn't it?" Michaels asked. The analogy was accurate; arm the common man, and you can take down an army.

"Mmmh. Looks that way. " I pondered the scene for a moment, then turned to my friend and asked, "Now, how do we get them on our side?'

Michaels thought for a moment, using his

skills in psychology and criminology to assess the crowd. "Well, right now the people with the guns are the ones giving out all the candy. Shiny, new, deadly candy, but candy all the same. What we need is ..."

"Sweeter candy." I jumped in, completing his sentence. He was right. The crowd may have been full of adults, but these were not normal people. No matter if their poison was Alcohol, Crack, Jack, Zip, or plain old Meth, they all had a carrot that could be dangled in front of them. And any of the ones who were here suffering in the Zone by no fault of their own, would likely go along with the crowd not only for their own safety, but to find their niche and fit in, no matter what.

Before I had taken the initial mission here in Miami, I performed a ritual of sorts. I sat down with my mother, my Aunt Chele, and my grandfather, and looked through old photos with them. Since Granddad had been sick, we all met in his hospital room, finding space around the IV drips and beeping machines, and remembering times both good and bad. Granddaddy's collection of photographs was impressive to say the least. As a little girl, he taught me to line up a shot, to crop an image, and to show small pieces of life around us, not to ignore what was out of the frame, but to show in sharp focus what really needed to be seen. I don't know why it all clicked back in at that moment, as it had often in my years with the FBI, but every time Granddaddy's photography lessons helped me focus on a needed detail, I was more and more proud of the lessons he had taught me.

"When I was getting the girls out of the Zone the last time, we went through the warehouse by Pier 23. Almost got stuck in a crossfire between two rival gangs. If Grummold's' men hadn't come in and put a stop to it, those groups would have killed each other."

Aaron looked at me blankly, then looked around the crowd, still blinded to what was right in front of me. "I don't get it Ellie. How does that help us now?"

I pointed to some of the armed men who were still passing out weapons. "See those Blue-green tattoos on their necks and faces? They called themselves the 'Reeferistas'. From what I saw, they definitely did not get with the ones over there in the orange and purple shirts; they called themselves the 'Listillios'. They hated each other. Didn't take much to start them shooting to kill.

I could see Michaels internal wheels turning,

connecting the dots with the facts I laid before him. "And there are lots of brand spanking new weapons just itching to be used, right here and now."

"Only question I have is, how do we get 'em started?" I asked Aaron, crossing my arms and slouching back down to think. Aaron didn't need time to think though. He tussled his hair, pulled half his shirt out of his pants, and left my side. Before I could stop him, he had walked over close to one of the groups of Listillios and started a dialogue with himself, loud enough to be heard by those close by, and convincingly crazy enough to not be questioned.

"Damned Reeferistas!" He exclaimed, hitting himself on the chest as he staggered by one of the opened, empty crates and started to rummage through it. "They give us all the guns, but they keep the BIG stuff for themselves!" He was sporting a vaguely Puerto Rican accent, and the dirt still on his face from the swim into the Zone added a colouring to his skin and a scent to his frame that made it seem like he belonged here. "and the good stuff too, " he added, swatting a Listillio nearby on the shoulder. "Man, you should have seen the Zip they carried into that place. Talk about the trip of a lifetime!" Michaels then laughed loud, and lo and behold, the Listillios started laughing with him. Within two minutes, he

142

was the focus of attention for at least twenty gang members who were *very* interested in the tales of drugs and superguns to be found in a 'poorly guarded, rickety building, just one street over'. I listened as best I could as they tested him, casually checking his story for falsehood. Never once did he falter, nor let his guard down. After ten minutes, I could almost see the sly grins forming on the gang members faces. Michaels knew when his job was done, and he soon after let his 'crazy' act take him diving into a nearby dumpster looking for more *gold* as he put it. I could hear him clearly on my comm as he whispered, "Think they bought it?"

The gang members were gathering in front of the empty crates, relaying the El Dorado-like tale to those who were just arriving. "Yep" I answered back, adding, "Let's get around to the back of my girls, and wait for the fireworks. If this doesn't draw away the guards, I don't know what will."

14
❧Wishes❧

Ever wish for something so hard, that you found yourself grinding your teeth when thinking about it, only to get what you wanted and think, *'Gee, that wasn't what I expected!'* The bullets flying around my head said pretty much that. Michaels' deception had indeed caught the attention of the Listillios, and just like we'd hoped, they soon launched an all-out offensive on the run-down brick building that held my girls captive. A small assault team burst from the front entrance to directly engage the Listillios, and the haphazard marksmanship of each side sent bullets and tracers flying in all directions. Michaels and I had to hide and watch, just to keep from being hit.

From the back alley, Michaels and I had no choice but to hole up, and we waited until Grummold's guards were drawn from the back of the building to the firefight at its entrance. Once we had the chance, we slid across the now empty alley, dodging stray bullets and still trying hard to not be seen. After reaching the decaying brick wall, we followed the structure away from the guards and gunslingers until we found a broken basement window. Michaels took look out as I slid through and down. I could feel the sharp edges of the broken glass trying to rip into the armourweave, but each time an edge caught, the weave held true and the glass broke away, leaving me unharmed. We both took our turns going thru the narrow frame, and splashed down into a basement half-filled with green, algae-laden water. The room had apparently been flooded for some time, and become a cesspool. Michaels took a flashlight from one of his pouches, and forcibly hit the base of it on the low ceiling, making it attach so we could assay the space. Of course we couldn't see the floor, and even with the light shining overhead, the water was either too deep or too murky to get the faintest inkling of its volume. Boxes and crates, old filing cabinets, and other assorted junk lined the walls, and across from our point of entry we could see a door; one of those old wooden doors that had once held a frosted glass pane. The glass was mostly gone now, and the rippling water made the shadows from our flashlight dance down the partially visible hallway. It was impossible to tell if we were seeing movement, or just an illusion of movement. Aaron pulled down the flashlight and stuck it back in his pack, handing me a small set of light-screen goggles and donning another pair himself. The tech involved with these worked very well for short periods of time, but they were far from perfect. Last time I had worn these was back in the Dark Zone in Mobile, and they overheated on me when I needed them most, leaving me blind in the middle of a nasty situation. All things considered though, the light screens didn't cast light away from us, so Aaron and I would be able to move through the dark spaces of the building without throwing up a signal that we were coming.

The noise from the attack out front helped us pinpoint our direction as we carefully crept along the dark stairway and corridors. The walls were rotting sheetrock, and showing signs of mold coming up through what was left of the paint that covered them. Of all the buildings I had been in here in Miami, this one was one of the oldest. Most of the infrastructure that had been lost to the Miami Dark Zone had been built in the reconstruction from the Hurricanes of the early nineteen nineties, but not this place. The architecture was easily over one hundred years old, and the whole structure had that World War II, film noir look about it. If I had closed my eyes, and opened them to find the world had turned to black and white, I don't think it would have surprised me.

Of course, old buildings like this had been remodeled and reorganized dozens of times since their initial construction, so hallways that once were straight and true were now rambling, disheveled mazes that often lead to dead ends or collapsed walls. Despite this, I had a pretty good idea of how to get to the girls; the dragonfly had mapped the first few floors for us. We even had a plan to get out. The fire escapes weren't accessible from the street level, but we sure as hell could use them to get down and away. If each of us carried a little girl, we could make it down and find some quick shelter, then get out of the Zone for good.

Only twice did we have to jump back to keep from being seen by guards who were running towards the front of the building, no doubt to act as reinforcements. The gang members were doing their part, even if unwittingly. As long as they kept it going, we had a good chance of getting out of here alive with my girls.

Many years before, I had learned that time is meaningless. It is a concept that we measure with fine precision, yet is fleeting and variable beyond measure. When bored, five minutes feels like fifty.

147

The converse is true when excited, as the old saying *'Time flies when you are having fun"* would tell you. But the human experience is filled with more than fun and boredom. Each of our passions has its own subtle nuance, and each combines in unexpected, illogical ways to create a new passion, with its own unique feeling. Being wrapped in your lovers arms, watching a fire burn as you laze together, with nothing more to do than be and exist and love can feel, at the time, like you have forever. When life kicks back in and steals that freedom from you, one realizes that you never have enough time, and what you had only whetted your appetite. You may measure time to the millionth of a second, but in the moment - no matter what the moment is - time is both fleeting and forever, and cannot be measured.

I could see the map from the dragonfly in my head, and I knew we had only one more floor to go before we would reach Erin and Olivia. The first floor went quickly; the second, not so much. Michaels told me that he thought the first floor took the longest. Somehow, I knew we were both right, and that it really didn't matter how long it took. Now we were closing in on the stairway to floor three, and we were getting close to my girls. Each step may as well have taken years, and that would have been no different had I been running and not sneaking.

The stairway to floor three was empty. Most places here had either been used to store items, people, or trash, but not here. While parts of this building were filth-laden abominations, others were obviously well-used. Floor three was also well lit, allowing Michaels and I to turn off our light-screens and tuck them away. I covered the top of the stairs while Aaron covered the rear, making sure no one came up behind us, but we both knew that if someone *had* discovered us, the ensuing fight would alert everyone to the fact that we were here. At that moment, I really considered myself lucky that I had just turned twenty-eight. If Michaels and I had been older agents, we would have gone through our training without the revamped Urban Tactics courses that were now required. We essentially received four weeks of the same high intensity training that Navy Seals were given. Parts of that training now covered what my Granddaddy referred to as the "Zombie Apocalypse" scenario, where hiding and stealth were important not because someone else was trying to shoot you, but because some*thing* else wanted to eat you alive. Here and now, standing in the old stairwell, not sure what was at the top, surrounded by the sound of gunfire outside and the smell of mold, decay and death inside, that scenario was coming true. I leapt from the second step, up into the landing and placed my back towards a wall, finding that no one was guarding the top of the stars. Michaels followed less gracefully, almost tripping on the top step. Now that we were up, we could continue to cover each other. If the map in my head was still correct, my girls were only three rooms away.

The well-lit corridors here had been upgraded with modern materials and flooring. If I didn't know better, I'd swear we had somehow been transported to one of the 'newer' buildings. Faux marble tile and aluminum lined sheetrock were the theme here, with low energy lighting bright enough to read by. "Perhaps the building wasn't as weak as we had thought," I whispered to Michaels, who nodded in agreement. The falling-down brick facade was as fake as the act that Michaels had used to trick the Listillios into attacking the place. It also explained why it was so well guarded: this was more than a place to hold the girls, this was looking more and more like Grummold's headquarters.

We hit the end of the hallway and quickly turned to survey the next room, Pulsers at the ready. This room was laid out like a modern office, with networking equipment and computer terminals linked up to run Grummold's interest. Michaels approached one of the massive towers and reached into one of his pouches, pulling out a small black square and magnetically attaching it to the back of the tower.

"Might as well do this while we can Ellie." Michaels said with a wink. "Gets us a foot in the electronic door. Zim? You getting anything?"

"Hell yea!" Zimmerman responded in our earpieces. "Signal is strong, and I am getting a good data feed. Most of this isn't even encrypted. There should be enough here to..."

Zimmerman was cut off by voices from the next room. A quick *"Shh"* was all he needed to mute his end of the commlink so Michaels and I could think. We stooped down next to the closest computer rack while two armed men passed. They had come from the direction of the girls, and headed slowly down the stairs we had just come up. After they had gone, I looked down the hallway toward a partially opened door, and I could see a small foot laying in the doorway. My first impulse was to forget all my training, and sprint as fast as I could to go hold them close, but as much as I wanted to give into that impulse, I couldn't - not yet. Losing it here and now would be a quick way to make sure that none of us made it out alive.

Even working hard to keep my calm, the girls were like a magnet, pulling me towards them. Each step down the hallway felt like an invisible hand was pushing me, pulling me, and I had to force myself to slow down. The short hall felt like it was miles long, but Michaels and I finally reached the door. I peeped in carefully and could clearly see my girls. Erin was propped up against the wall, her eyes partially opened, but rolled back in unconsciousness. Olivia had a large bruise on her left eye, and aside from the wet clothes from her earlier accident, looked otherwise unharmed. Both were bound with tie wire, and Chester was stuffed between them. I took a quick look around the room, and holstered my Pulser, finally taking the steps forward and reaching my girls. They both felt cold, and for one moment, my heart stopped. I couldn't tell if they were breathing, and in that tiny fraction of time, I thought they were dead. I could see myself just sitting there, crying silent tears, letting the men who had taken them from me find us, and take my life. For the eternity of that moment, I didn't care if I lived or died. A little wiggle from Olivia brought me back to the moment, and I took my multitool from its place in my armourweave and cut them both free. Olivia tried to speak, but whatever they had drugged her with kept anything more than a slurred hint of speech from leaving her mouth. My Erin was still out cold, but now that I was here, I knew she'd be OK.

Michaels bent down to grab Erin, and started to lift when the taser bolt hit him from across the room, sending small blue sparks from his exposed flesh where it hit. He crumpled to the floor almost instantly, his cries of pain still echoing in the room after he'd blacked out. I turned, drawing my Pulser, and having it immediately kicked from my hand. Grummold stepped out from the shadows, leveling the taser at my head, and holding up a federal issue homing beacon that he must've taken from inside Chester.

"I was wondering when you'd get here." he said, as he re-aimed at my neck and pulled the trigger, sending Zeus' thunderbolt through my body, and plummeting me into an agony that too late brought its darkness.

15
☙Passage☙

Some people think that sleep is equal to being unconscious, but in my experience, there is a vast difference. For one, sleep is, for the most part, something you actively take part in. Even while your body rests, your brain is full of activity, creating dreams, spinning nightmares, and engaging itself on a level that it cannot when the body is awake. Sleep is, above all else, a natural part of living.

Unconsciousness is something completely different, and as with most things, there is more than one type. When I was five, and had to have a minor valve correction in my heart, they 'put me to sleep.' Despite my young age, I remember vividly the feeling that, when I woke up, I had lost something irreplaceable. I was out of sync with the universe, and the time I was out was gone to me forever. The pain and soreness in my body was nothing compared to the fright I felt having simply dropped off the planet for six hours. When I was older, in college, and fairly stupid as most of us are, I drank on one or two occasions to the point of blacking out. Upon waking, I felt that same sense of lost time, of being out of sync. In one case I was with friends. In the other, I was not, and I realized quickly how lucky I was to have not been violated, or die in some awful way when I lost consciousness. Small differences in hindsight, but at the moment of waking, when you don't know where you are, how long you've been out, and sometimes aren't even sure *who* you are, those differences define your entire world.

I was aware of sounds before I could find the strength to open my eyes. The gunfight was no longer going on outside, and I could only assume the Listillios had either been dispersed or slaughtered. With one ear on the floor, I could hear the hum and bump of sound and activity on the level below. It was then that I realized my face was lying flat on the ground, and my arms were bound behind my back. I moved slightly and received a jolt from the wire that held me. Grummold sat a few feet away from me, talking on his comm. He was wheeling and dealing, and Michaels and I were his newest commodity.

155

"Yes, I imagine you will enjoy breaking her. She's spirited and strong, and should be quite a lot of fun." The sound of the man's voice almost made me vomit; he could have been reading Shakespeare, and it would have sounded slimy and revolting. I suppressed the bile in my throat as he continued, "Yes, yes, of course we can have her prepared if you wish. If you would rather have her as a doll, we can begin the lobotimization immediately. Of course, that is one hundred thousand credits extra, and you must realize there are no guarantees. Money is up front, and if she dies in the process, then I hope you like Necrophilia. As you desire, sir. As soon as the monetary transfer is complete, we will begin."

Grummold looked down and noticed my open eyes as he cut the communication. "Well, well, little girl." he seethed, reaching out his four and a half fingered hand and stroking my hair. "I almost didn't recognize you. Black hair and Olive skin looked better on you, I would say, but my client has decided he has a new preference. He likes them pale; pale and cold." He spat on me as he pulled his hand away. "Personally, I hope you die during the lobotomy."

"Where are my girls?" I managed to say, a small tremble in my voice showing my physical state.

"Your girls? They were *never* your girls. They were mine to do with as I chose, and you stole them. Now I have all three of you. The girls have already been sold. Only delivery has yet to be set, but do not worry; they do have a wonderful time ahead of them. O'kasa Colony has a taste for them young."

Terror hit me with an almost uncontrollable force. O'kasa Colony was offshore, just outside US jurisdiction and in international waters. It was a man-made island run by a multinational conglomerate that believed that by giving into your primal instincts, you could become an improved human. There had been rumors for years about everything from genetic experimentation to cannibalism. The thought of my little girls going to a place like that was almost too much to bear.

"And Aaron? What have you done to him?"

Grummold chuckled as he leaned closer. "He is of no real use to me, but I have an acquaintance in Peru who is always in need to good stock for his tests. Your friend will be divvied up among the South American Medical community for experimentation."

"You rotten son of a..." I started, but Grummold cut me off with a kick to the head.

"How dare you curse me! I only got twenty-five thousand for him! He's hardly worth the trouble!"

Grummold turned to walk away, shutting the door behind him. I could hear him back on his comm through the door, demanding to know if the money transfer had been completed for my sale so they could lobotomize me. His scream of anger told me the answer was no, and I could hear him tear off down the hall to tend to 'other business'.

16
❧Maimed❧

I struggled to find enough energy to move, and after five minutes managed to roll onto my back, pressing my hands painfully together between my body and the floor. Looking over, I could see my girls. No one had moved them. They had only been two feet away from me the whole time. I rolled my head to the other side and found that Aaron was tied down by the far wall. Aside from the four of us and a small desk, the room was empty.

A shift of my body weight caused the tie wire around my wrist to respond with another electric shock. I fought the urge to cry out, and settled myself into a grotesque angle that hurt my back, but kept the tie wire from reacting to me with a shock. The room itself now was quiet. Not the calm quiet that allows one to think clearly, but the oppressive silence that fills the air, making it heavy and hard to breathe. My own voice seemed muted when I called out, "Aaron? Aaron, can you hear me?"

He stirred a bit, getting a shock from the ties that held him. Once he settled down and the electricity stopped flowing through him, he looked around and surveyed the situation. "Any way you can get over here Ellie?" he asked quietly. He was only ten or eleven feet away from me, but each move caused more raw power to jolt through me, draining what little strength I had built back up.

I lay on the floor, turning my head so I could see my girls, and felt a tear roll down from my eye. I wasn't prone to crying, or giving up, but seeing these sweet children, and knowing that I had failed to keep them safe was almost too much for me. The first tear was followed by another. I looked back up at the ceiling as the tears started to flow, each one steadily marching down my face. Some of the tears found their way into my ear, stifling my hearing in the already oppressive quiet.

Then I heard a pop, followed by static. Then another pop, and the faintest call of "Ellie? El, can you hear me?" Zimmerman's voice was once again coming thru the hidden comm I still wore. I whispered a response. "Zim? Zim, where have you been?"

The connection was still full of static, but grew stronger as he spoke. "I heard Grummold, then a pop, and silence. What happened?"

"Taser shot, point blank." I answered. "I thought for sure the electricity would have shorted out the comms."

"Well, for whatever reason, yours is working now. Catch me up - how screwed are you, and what can I do to help?"

I took a few minutes to relay our situation to Zim, all the while hearing him relay the info to Director Forrest. When I got to the part about being tied up with electric tie wire, Forrest cursed loudly. They decided to keep the comm link open so we wouldn't risk it going down again, and stepped away to work on a solution.

I took a deep breath and held it, throwing my body weight into a roll across the floor, and fighting thru the pain of the tie wire. It only took me a few seconds to reach Michaels this way, but that was long enough that the wire had started burning my wrists, and I could smell the horrid stench of roasted human as it wafted through the air. I probably would have thrown up if there had been anything left in my stomach to expel, but a few dry heaves were all I could muster. Aaron's hands were tied behind him as well, so he wouldn't be able to help me escape any more than I could currently help him. He'd passed out again from his struggle against the tie wires, and my girls were still out cold. All I had accomplished was to reach the other side of the room, but from this angle, I could see the backside of the desk. It was a typical old, small aluminum desk, but over here, I could see a rusted, torn edge that was not visible from my vantage point earlier. I rolled again over to the desk, working hard to ignore the pain that was lessened now because of my burned skin. Sitting up was another struggle, as was placing my back against the desk and finding the rough edge by feel rather than by sight. The desk worked as a ground of sorts, lessening the waves of electricity from the tie wires, and after a few minutes of working my arms up and down across the desk, the thin wire finally gave way, and my hands were free.

It only took me a few seconds to reach into the armourweave and find a multitool to cut my legs free, then over to Michaels. He awoke just as I tipped him over to free his hands, nearly hitting his head on the floor. Michaels immediately reached into his armourweave and pulled out the tracker we'd used to map the building, but found that the taser shot had fried it. His comm was dead too. I un-muted the channel on my comm, but I didn't have time to update Zim with anything more than a "*Zim, we're free - will keep you posted*", before cutting him off.

From what I could remember of the map we'd made with the Dragonfly, just up the hall, through the computer room, and to the left was a room with a window, and that window had a fire escape. Aaron and I quickly went over an escape plan, and I stayed to ready the girls while he checked the getaway route, and silenced anyone who would potentially be in our way. I heard the muffled "pheung" of a Pulser shot hitting its target, then the same again. Within three minutes Michaels came back into the room, and I passed him Olivia. She'd almost come to when I moved her, and groggily cried out for Chester. I handed the old rabbit to her and she curled up in Aaron's arms, going right back to the uneasy, drug induced sleep she'd been in for God knows how long. Aaron staggered a bit under Olivia's weight, still drained from the tie wire that had been pouring electricity into his body.

"You go ahead Aaron. Get her out of here. I'll

follow you with Erin." Michaels nodded, understanding that it was not a request, and headed out of the room towards the escape. I knelt beside Erin, placing my hands under her legs and against her back, and started to lift, too late realizing that she was tied to the floor by her belt loops. The jolt woke her, and she looked through hazy eyes, and smiled.

"I knew you'd come for us Ellie." Erin almost jumped into my arms, hugging me tight. We simply held each other for a moment before she asked, "Where's Livy?"

"My friend Aaron went ahead with her. Now, we're going to get you out of here, young lady," I said, giving her the same smile my Nana and Mama Jerri had always given me. I took my multitool out and reached behind her to clip the wires that held her down, then lifted Erin with a new-found strength. Erin hooked her hands together, and tossed them around my neck, holding on and nestling in as I carefully stepped down the hallway, through the computer room, and then out to the room on the left. As I entered the room that had the fire escape, a taser bolt shot right by my head, barely missing me and burying itself in the wooden doorframe with a hiss, throwing off blue sparks and causing Erin to scream.

Grummold stood across from the open window, reloading the taser. I drew my Pulser with my free hand, only to find that my hours in the darkness had left it too drained to fire. I slowly put Erin down and asked, "Love, can you walk?"

"I think so Ellie," she answered, straightening out her wobbly legs and reaching for the wall to steady herself.

"Then you go hide, my love. I'll come find you when I am done here."

She answered a well-behaved "Yes ma'am." and scooted back the way we came, leaving Grummold and I to face off alone.

"Let us go, Grummold. You can't have them, or me."

Grummold stood across the room, glaring at me with a hatred I had rarely seen. "My men will find the other girl and your friend. I can get ten thousand for him dead, so either way, he is a non-issue. YOU are now worth more to me dead than alive." With this, Grummold reached into his jacket and pulled out the hand cannon I had seen him use to kill Strong-Arm. I hardly had time to react as he pulled the trigger, the armor piercing shell going through the weave of my top and through my left shoulder. I felt the bullet slam into my armourweave from the inside, and exit my body, nearly spinning me around.

Adrenaline was kicking in now, as was my training, and I rushed Grummold before he could re-aim. My left arm was useless, but I still had my legs, and the kickboxing lessons I had started when I was twelve. With a quick spin and jump, I removed the gun from Grummold's hands and sent it across the room. I could tell from the brief contact my leg had with his arm that despite his portly, less than formidable appearance, he was all muscle and sinew, and would not be easy to take down, especially since I was losing blood and already weak from the multitude of electric shocks I had endured. Grummold rushed me, arms stretched out for my neck, and suddenly I couldn't breathe. He had both his hands cutting off my circulation and oxygen, and I was feeling faint already. One well-placed head-butt was all I had the time to try, and it sent Grummold stumbling back, allowing me a moment to breathe again and move before his next attack.

Grummold's face was turning beet red, and I could tell that, strong as he may be, he wasn't used to the physical exertion of a one on one fight. I charged him again, this time planting a kick on his right cheek, but even as he fell, he grabbed my legs and twisted, throwing me into a spin and crashing to the floor myself. Suddenly, I felt my strength leave me, just for a moment. I was faltering, and despite Grummold's next attack spurring me to move faster than I thought I could, I couldn't keep this fight up much longer.

Fighting Grummold was like fighting an Ox. He didn't have my skill, or my speed, but he was big, thick, and solid. Blows that would have easily taken down other men had little effect on him, and I was left with a move that I had been taught never to use, unless I wanted to kill my opponent. I found my footing, took a flying leap at him, and kicked him full force with the ball of my foot right over his heart, causing it to briefly stop, then stutter. I'd nearly broken my ankle hitting him this way, but Grummold fell to his knees, gasping for breath and grabbing his chest. I stood over him, my back to the glass windows that lead to my exit, and looked down on him as he lay dying. With blood on his lips, Grummold managed to say, "I still win, little girl. Let my spite kill you now."

My stomach seized when he said this. I knew

from my time working in the Zones that spite was a black market explosive, designed to kill an opponent after you die. I looked down as Grummold gave his last convulsion, then back up through the darkened door where Erin had gone to hide. Grummold's body exploded in what felt like slow motion, the force of the blow sending me back through the glass windows, and over the fire escape rail toward the ground. As I fell, I could see the fireball erupt from the third floor window, burning up everything. I reached out before I hit the ground, futilely calling her name.

Erin was gone.

17
❧Ether❧

I was looking through the burned out building, surveying the damage, and searching. There was still a haze over my eyes, like a thin sheet of translucent film was somehow being worn over them, blurring my vision only slightly. The whole side of the third floor was gone, opening up to ground zero for the blast the almost killed me. The rest of the floor hadn't fared much better. Partially melted computer racks and destroyed cores filled the next room. Each one would have made a good place for a little girl to hide, but no sign of her remains had yet been located. I shifted through the rubble of the computer room, and looked down the hallway, noticing the hall floors still shown bright and polished.

"Anyone check the holding room yet?" I asked Gallindo. He looked up from his work and briefly surveyed the hall.

"Not that I know of Ellie. Why don't you check it out?'

Gallindo went back to his work picking tiny shards of data discs out of the remains of a tower, and I stood, the rush of blood muffling my hearing, to head toward the short hallway and the room where my girls and I had been held. Reaching the door, I found its surface smooth and unscarred by the flames that had destroyed the rest of this floor. Its doorknob still gleamed as polished brass should, distant lights dancing off its surface, begging for me to open the door. As I did so, Gallindo and his men vanished behind me, and I was alone. I pushed the door opened to see a little girl in a pink running suite, long hair flowing down her back, partially turned away from me, and playing with a stuffed rabbit that was black with soot and ash.

"Erin?" I asked.

She nodded yes, then asked, "Why didn't you get me Ellie?"

With this, the girl turned to face me, her charred cheeks breaking apart as she moved, and her eyes still gleaming, unharmed by the fire.

"You promised you'd come get me Ellie. Where did you go?"

I fell to my knees, unable to look away from the child before me, tears failing to come; only deep heaving sobs filled my lungs. She reached out to take my hand, small burned portions of her skin crumbling away as she did so.

"You promised Ellie."

It was the same dream I'd had a hundred times since waking in St. Augustine's a week ago. One month had now passed since I lost Erin to Grummold's spite, three weeks of which I had been unconscious. Odd that I didn't feel like I had lost time, but I knew I had lost something much more dear to me.

The stark white walls of the hospital room glowed in the sunlight that poured through the large window that looked out onto New Miami. I had only stood a handful of times since waking, and even then only for a few minutes, but as I grew stronger, I found myself gingerly making my way over to the window, and starring out, deep in an empty thought, and reliving the last moments over and over again. I was lucky to be alive from what I had been told. Not only had Grummold's bullet missed anything important, but I had only cracked the back of my skull, and a few ribs when I landed.

I sat next to the window, looking out and trying hard not to think too much. I was still on a lot of medication to handle the pain caused not only by my injuries, but by the other medications I was taking to spur on the knitting of my bones. The bullet wound had been stitched up when I was still unconscious, and healed up pretty well. One small scar was the only outward sign I had to show for it. On the inside, I felt like there was nothing left but scars, and I'd never be the same person again.

Around three o'clock, Forrest and Michaels came to check in on me. I had only seen them briefly since I regained consciousness, and as much as I just wanted to lie down and mourn Erin, the investigator in me had too many questions to let my brain settle down for long. I still didn't know what had happened to Olivia, or even how I had gotten out of the Zone in the first place. Today was not an official visit; there would be no deposition, and no debriefing. Today was about bringing us together, so we could move on together.

I was shocked when Forrest opened the door, and held it for Michaels, who entered hobbling about with a cane.

"Aaron? What in the world did you do?" I asked, almost afraid to find out. His left leg was in an old-fashioned cast, and *that* had tubes attached to micro-pumps and smallish IV bags, adding in whatever chemical concoction was needed for his leg.

"Eh, it's not that bad Ellie." Michaels shuffled around to sit on the edge of my bed, and propped his cane up against my nightstand. Before he continued, he leaned over and gave me a gentle hug, and kissed the side of my face. Forrest hugged me too before he sat.

"Where's Zim?" I inquired, noting his absence.

"Zimmerman is stuck back in Mobile doing some clean-up work for this whole Miami situation." Forrest answered, fiddling with his handheld computer. "He wanted to be here, but considering that you are being transferred back home to Mobile in a day or so, we told him to wait and see what he could do to get everything in order."

I nodded, knowing full well that I'd rather have him here with me than back home in Mobile tying up loose ends. Sometimes you just had to go with a situation, and be OK with whatever comes along. Considering that I was lucky to be alive, that was my game plan for the foreseeable future.

"Where's Olivia?" I asked, suddenly not able to meet my friends' eyes. "Does she know?"

Aaron reached out and gave my shoulder a small squeeze. "She knows, but she's not saying anything - to anyone, actually. She sits in her padded room, and won't talk to anyone but that rabbit."

I felt an unrestrained tear force its way from my eye, and run down my cheek. "How did we get out, Aaron?" As much as I didn't want to know the details, I knew I could never let it go if I didn't know.

Aaron turned a bit white and looked away from me, out the window over New Miami, then down to the floor. Forrest moved a bit closer and spoke quietly.

"You hit the ground Ellie, but Aaron was watching for you. He came out of hiding and pulled you out of the alleyway, while the Listillios saw the explosion and ran. Some of their cover fire went stray, and hit Michaels in the leg." Forrest gestured to Aarons' wounded left leg and took a deep breath. "He carried you and Olivia away from Grummold's place, and back toward Pier 23. I don't know how he got that far, but when he was trying to lower you two down to a retrieval boat I'd sent in..."

"Wait. Retrieval boat? I thought the Zone was closed?"

Forrest held up his hand, saying "One tale at a time, Ellyandra. As I was saying, Aaron was trying to lower you two down to the rescue boat, and he fell into the water. You know how putrid that water is, Ellie, and all that funk and nastiness went right into his bloodstream. Not only was he poisoned, but he almost lost that leg."

Aaron rejoined the conversation, adding "Well, I didn't lose it, and haven't yet. Docs think that most of the bone they had to cut out will re-grow within a few months. I'll be fine."

"You'll be decorated." Forrest said, then added, "And you will like it, and you will accept the commendation. Understood?"

Aaron sheepishly nodded, answering a quiet "Yes Sir" before he turned to look out the window again. This time, I worked to stand, and reached over to Michaels, putting my arms around his neck, and planting a big kiss on his cheek. "Thank you for getting me out Aaron."

"El, you'd have done the same for me. That's what we do."

"Yes," I replied, sitting back down before I fell down. "but we are always grateful."

****

Three more days passed before they would discharge me from St. Augustine's, and in that time my strength started to return. I was up on my own two feet by Saturday morning, and instead of transferring me to Providence in Mobile, I was being sent home, with a visiting nurse set to check on me every few hours. Zim had made sure that all my house systems were up and running, and set to monitor me for any problems, and Forrest flew ahead to tend to any last minute issues with the medical leave I would have to take. Michaels stayed in Miami with me, and helped me gather what few belongings I had for the flight home.

"Aaron, there's one more thing I need to do before I go home." I muttered, stuffing a night gown into my luggage.

"She hasn't said a word to anyone Ellie. Why do you think you have a chance to get anything out of her?

I grabbed the nearest item (an old hardback book my granddaddy had sent me) and threw it at Aaron. " It's not about what I can get from her! It's about what she needs from me!" I sat down on the bed, my heart starting to race with emotion. "She's lost everything Aaron. She at least needs to know that I tried. Even if that doesn't help her now, one day maybe it will."

We finished our work in silence, Michaels making the half dozen trips down to the parking level and the unmarked FBI vehicle that waited to take me to the airport. Finally, discharge papers in hand, he came up to my room with the required wheelchair and I sat, feeling helpless, and strangely alone. As soon as we hit the front door, I held up my hand to stop the forward movement of the chair, and rose from it, determined to leave this place on my own two feet, even if the steps were awkward, as the distance from the chair to the waiting car was short. I pulled the passenger door closed, and waited for Aaron to hop into the back seat. Imagine my surprise when he showed up at the driver's door, relieving the agent who'd been assigned to drive us to the airport, and hopped behind the steering wheel.

We pulled out from St. Augustine's, and onto the streets of New Miami. Within minutes, we'd reached the Safeway entrance, and the enhanced roadway system took control of the car. Aaron released the wheel, allowing the computer to take command, all the while starring forward through the front windshield and off into the distance. After we'd been merged into traffic, the vehicle computer spoke, asking for our destination.

"Miami Children's Hospital, please." I turned to look at Aaron as the computer plotted our course, a large smile uncontrollably building on my lips.

"Thank..." was all I got out before he interrupted.

"Don't thank me Ellie. I couldn't leave her sitting there either; not without trying. I figure it's like it was the first time. If anyone is going to get her to talk, it'll be you."

****

Miami Children's Hospital had been nationally recognized for decades as one of the best children's facilities in the country. Its position next to the Safeways had not quite been its downfall. Unlike most cities where the border around the Safeways and the new cities was a virtual no man's land, Miami was different. The multi-floored hospital building sat in the shadow of New Miami, but they had continued to work over the years to make sure their physical position didn't impede their goal, which had remarkably remained humanitarian driven.

After the Safeway had delivered us to the proper exit, Michaels took control of the vehicle again, and we soon found ourselves parking out in front of the old Hospital, and getting the needed passes to visit Olivia.

We were led into a basement level, where no sunlight would reach us. The bright fluorescent lighting was outdated, and cast a sickly pallor over everyone it fell upon. The orderly, an elderly African

America named Chuck, led us down and around and through the twisted corridors.

"Why do they have her here, Chuck?" I asked quietly.

"Oh, she's been good for the most part; they're just afraid that she might decide to hurt herself." he said, passing me her admission report. "It's for her own good."

As we walked down the hallways, and to another set of stairs, I remembered my mother telling me that the nasty tasting medicine was always for my own good, as were the shots, the lessons, and a hundred other damned things that felt like they were breaking my heart at the time. In retrospect, she had been right about almost all of it. I still questioned the purgatives.

We reached the lower level, and headed down yet another hall, giving me a chance to read the report Chuck had passed to me. Finally, after several long minutes, we reached Olivia's door. Chuck rattled his keys on the ring. He took his time pulling out one and placing it in the lock, putting his thumbprint on the scanner as he did so. A resounding click filled the otherwise empty corridor, echoing off into the bowels of the facility, and I took a hard gulp of air before I stepped into the room.

The fluorescent lights poured an almost blinding light into the stark white room from over twelve feet above. Rubber padding covered the walls, and the floor even gave with each step, cushioning my footfalls. There was almost nothing in here: a small stoop jutted from the wall to act as a toilet, but it too was covered in such a way that no one could hurt themselves on it. There was no bed, only a small cushy pallet laid on the floor. The light above made all this white glow with a surrealistic aura. Olivia was sitting in the middle of the floor, her back turned to the door, her healthy pink skin radiating where it poked through her white gown. She turned her head to look at me, then turned back to Chester, whose dingy fur set his out from the rest of the room. I moved slowly towards Olivia, and knelt gently beside her. Still she played silently with Chester, not ignoring me, but refusing to say a word.

"Livy?" I asked quietly, my voice seeming to thunder in the oppressive silence that filled the room. Moments passed before she responded at all. Even then, she simply made Chester look at me, then back to her and shake his head no. I knew it was abnormal, but I had an idea that might help her bridge the gap.

"Chester?' I asked, calling out the rabbit. She immediately turned his head back to me, tilted quizzically as if to say "*yeusss?*". Olivia herself still looked away, unable to raise her head to meet my eyes.

"Chester, honey. I am so glad you are OK. I was worried about you." At this Chester shook his head no, and turned his back to me. The little girl was an excellent puppeteer, and his nuanced movements gave up the secrets her heart still held. If I paid attention to Chester, I'd know what she couldn't bring herself to say.

"Chester." I pined. "Please don't be that way. I got here as fast as I could. I was in the hospital, and they just let me go today."

With this, Chester turned his head back to me, and ever so slightly, Olivia shifted her body so she could move Chester over close to me, and have him pat me on the leg. He hung his little head now just like Olivia, ears flopping over his face in sorrow, and settled in between us. I reached over to put my arm around Olivia, but she flinched as soon as I moved, so I placed my arm around Chester instead. The stuffed rabbit started to move and jerk in the closest approximation to crying as he could, and all I could do was pat him on the back, stroke his threadbare fur and tell him it would be OK.

In my mind's eye, I could see Erin standing in the white room with us, eyes glowing a healthy blue and white against her burned skin. I could hear her say, *"You promised, Ellie",* and I myself almost started to break again. God love her, Olivia somehow noticed, even without looking at me, and finally placed her small hand around my arm, leaning her head against me.

The smell of raspberries floated up to my nostrils from Olivia's hair. The staff at Miami Children's had taken good care of her physically, but it hadn't been easy. I had read her intake sheet after checking in and found why she was in a safe room; she'd thrown a tantrum to beat all tantrums on her admission, screaming for her sister and crying out for me. There had been no way for Aaron to keep her from seeing me, unconscious, burned and bleeding, as he had carried us through the zone towards safety. The sight of me in such a state coupled with Erin's absence had thrown her into a panic, and she'd hit hear noggin against a table in frustration. Despite her age, they had to restrain and sedate her for her own good.

Erin still hovered around us, and I started to wonder if she was in my mind, or if her spirit was there, haunting us both. *"Ellie, where were you? Why didn't you come?"* the small voice said, barely a whisper, each syllable taking its toll on me as I held the apparitions' twin.

"You promised, Ellie." The words rang clear this time, not from my mind, but from Olivia, cutting through me with a pain my heart could hardly handle. I didn't look at her; I couldn't look at her. I just placed my hand around her head, holding her close, and placed a kiss on the topknot she'd been given.

"I know honey. I really tried. And I am so sorry my love." The swelling in my throat was becoming almost impassable, and I could hardly breathe, but there was nothing in Heaven or Hell that would make me move away from my little girl, nothing that could make me break that connection, no matter how small. Time and space were all meaningless to me as we sat together in the little cell, and I would not let her go.

"What happened to my sister, Ellie?" Olivia quietly asked after almost half an hour. "Where is my sister?"

"She's gone, love. A very bad thing happened, and she's gone." As I said this, I looked over to Erin's ghost, now standing in the corner by the toilet. The shadows' eyes closed briefly, then she vanished. Somehow I knew I'd see more of her spectral form in the countless nightmares that lay ahead, but for now, all I could do was try and be strong, and heal so I could help Olivia heal. I opened my arms and Olivia crawled up into my lap, tears running down her face. Chester dropped to the floor as Olivia held onto me with both arms now, the fear and torment of the last few months finally catching up with her outside of her dreams, pouring unstoppably out of her. It was a baptism in tears, soaking me to the skin, and forcing me through a spiritual transformation. I held my little girl closer, and despite her pain and mine, our bond lifted my heart and soul, making my mind up once and for all, as if there had ever been any question.

I turned to look at Aaron, who had been waiting in the doorway. "Michaels, go get me the Social Worker. We have work to do."

18
❧Coping❧

I promised Olivia that I wouldn't leave her in the hospital alone, so instead of flying home, I called in a few favors and stayed with her that night. Chuck was kind enough to bring in a larger pallet, and the Head Administrator approved since I had made such a breakthrough with Olivia. I found out later that we had both dreamed of Erin that night, but for God's Grace, when Livy dreamed of her sister, she wasn't the charcoal encrusted version that I saw when I closed my eyes. For that, I was forever grateful.

It took us a week of wheeling and dealing to secure temporary custody, with the understanding that back home in Mobile, I had the support system needed to raise a child. My job was there, as were my friends (who were all at my job) and my family, old and in some cases infirmed, but they were there.

When we finally left Miami, it was late in the day, and the red-orange glow of the setting sun gave me a sense of peace. Olivia held my hand as we rode silently to the Airport, snuggling on Chester and still whispering in is ear. Somehow the old rabbit seemed tired now that he wasn't being operated by two little girls. We turned off the Safeway into the Airport drop-off area, and a few kind gentlemen in black and gold striped jumpsuits grabbed what little luggage we had and made sure we got to check in. Olivia was at first frightened of the full body scanning booth, until I went through and showed her that it didn't hurt.

"Erin would love that, Ellie." She said, then quietly stopped herself and stepped silently in for her scan. I took her hand in mine as she stepped out, and the tradesman handed Chester back to her. Being that he was made of stuffiness and fur, he had to go through the big scanner, just in case anyone had put anything inside him.

"You mean like Mr. Aaron did to him?" she asked, looking at the stitching on his back where we'd sewn him back up.

"Exactly like Mr. Aaron did to him, love. But sometimes..." I stopped myself from telling her that sometimes bad people put things on planes to hurt people. In some ways, Olivia was not as brave as her sister had been, and while I'd never hold that against her, I sure as hell wasn't going to do anything to give her reason to panic now.

"Sometimes what, Ellie?" she inquired, eager for me to finish my thought.

"Sometimes, my love," I answered, stooping down to look her in the eyes, "Sometimes people put candy inside stuffies, and there is no candy allowed unless you buy it on the plane."

My quick response rolled in one ear and right out the other as she pointed out of the large windows overseeing the airfield, past the lights and the holograms that led planes to safety, and right at the well-lit Super Jet that was going to bring us home.

"That's a big bird, Ellie." She said, almost unable to keep from gawking. "And we're gonna go inside?"

"Yep, just as sure as your name is Olivia Carter."

"Olivia Carter-*Dyett*" she corrected, adding, "and Master Chester Carter-Dyett." holding Chester up for a hug. I squeezed them both tight, then led them down the ramp to the terminal, and out to the last ramp to board the plane home.

****

Once we made it home, Olivia settled in quickly. My mother and my Aunt Chele spent the first week tending to both of us, since I was still healing from the broken and cracked bones, and Olivia had hit a lapse in her potty training. Only once did my mother start to take a stern voice with her on the matter, and I put that to an immediate stop.

"Granddaddy said you were three, am I right?" I asked, standing at the bathroom door with mom, watching Olivia, and holding my temper in check.

"And?" she responded coolly, "Olivia is four. What of it?"

I stepped closer to Mom and lowered my voce so Olivia wouldn't hear. "Didn't Granddaddy tell me that he had to literally rub your nose in it to get you to stop peeing behind the couch?"

Mom took a step back, eyes blinking at me before she stammered out a, "I didn't know he told you that!"

"He told me lots of things mom, and nothing you went through is anything like what Olivia has gone through. I love you, but you can either cut the kid some slack, or you can go home till later. Got it?"

Mom and I had few fights growing up, but we were both hard-headed as they come. When I first bought my home here and mom came to stay, we very quickly came to the conclusion that even though she was my mother, and I loved her very much, under this roof it was my rules, my way. Period. Mom shook her head, realizing that she had overstepped, and that I was right. The last thing Olivia needed now was someone else being harsh with her. What she needed now, above all else, was compassion and patience. She just needed to be loved.

It was at dinner that same night that the fit hit the shan, so to speak. Mom and I had cooked a roasted turkey, but somehow it was left in the oven too long. I have my suspicions that a little girl was eager to have dinner, and decided to turn the oven up to four hundred seventy five degrees so it would cook faster. Cook it did, and soon we had black smoke billowing from the kitchen. The house computer removed all the smoke after a scan showed the fire was isolated inside the oven, and after turning off the heat, the fire soon died down.

Our dinner was, as they say, toast. The inner portion of the breast and thighs were salvageable though, so we gathered everyone together at the table, and sat down to poke through the birds' remains for edible meat.

Olivia sat and starred at the turkey, unable to take her eyes off it. After a few minutes, my mother asked, "Honey, have you never seen a turkey before?" Olivia remained silent, but the ever-present Chester nodded a yes. As mom continued to cut, I heard a faint dripping sound coming from under the table. Looking down, I could see that Olivia had wet herself. It was now that I noticed big tears building in her eyes.

"Livy, honey? What's wrong?" I asked, adding, "No one is mad about the turkey, my love. You're not in trouble."

Olivia started to speak, then stopped. Her shoulders started to quiver and shake under the weight of her emotional pain. I went and put my arms around her, but there was no response. I wasn't pushed away, but at that moment, she was a thousand miles from the dinner table.

Finally, after several silent moments, she asked, "Is that what my sister looked like, Ellie?"

The question cut through me like a bullet, leaving a searing pain in its wake. Across the table, at an empty chair, Erin's ghost spoke in my head, saying *"Pretty much, Livy."* Then, turning her eyes to me, she said, *"You promised, Ellie. Where were you?"*

I couldn't speak as the specter sat, looking at me with those untouched eyes, then vanished as quickly as she had come. My Aunt Chele piped up, answering Olivia.

"No no, love. This is a bird, and it was born for us to eat. Your sister *is* a little girl, just like you. She has never looked like this, dear." Like any four year old would, Olivia seemed accepting of Chele's doubletalk, and then allowed my dear aunt to take her upstairs to clean her up. I was far worse for the incident, and even after Chele and Olivia came back downstairs for dinner, I couldn't eat a bite.

After that night, it seemed like I couldn't get away from Erin's voice in my head. Everywhere we went, I was reminded that I had indeed promised to get her to safety, and to keep her safe. Now I was doing that with Olivia, but my Erin was still gone. Michaels was the best psychologist I knew, but he was "too close" to the situation to be objective, and referred me to another Doctor at the Bureau. Weeks of talk and meds did no good, either boring me to tears, or dulling my senses to the point that I was afraid Olivia would need me, and I would be too messed up to respond. I'd already let one sister die, and no matter what kind of torture my life became, I wasn't about to endanger Olivia by not really being there. After another day and night hearing Erin's voice, I knew I only had one other thing to do; only one other person who may be able to help, before I went completely bonkers.

****

"She wanted to come meet you, you know." I said as I leaned over to kiss my grandfather on the forehead. "But I was afraid that all the machines and lines and such might upset her."

"Of course it would upset her." my grandfather responded. "She's four; I'm eighty-two and it upsets the hell out of me!" He'd grown back his goatee while I was in Miami, and it was as snow white now as his hair, which sat in a mess of curls on top of his head. Somehow, it looked like a fake Christmas tree that had been put away in a hurry, and now all the branches and needles were stuck in awkward angles that just didn't look quite right, no matter how hard you tried to smooth them.

"You can bring her by another time, my love." he interjected, bringing my wandering mind back to the here and now. Putting on his glasses, he looked at me closer, and added "You could have brought yourself though. What's wrong, Ellyandra?"

No matter how hard I had tried, I could never hide from Granddaddy's insight. When I was little, that small fact helped insure that I stayed in some degree of trouble. As I got older, it kept me from sneaking out and doing stupid things. I cursed the old man on more than one occasion for his almost gypsy-like skill at seeing what I was trying to hide. As I got older, I treasured him for it.

Before I knew it, I was telling him everything. About sneaking into the Dark Zone in Miami, finding the girls and starting a riot as cover. His face twisted in anger as I described their condition when I found them, and his monitors all started to go off in a frenzy when I told him how Grummold took us down and planned to sell us all. Twenty minutes, three coughing fits and several nurses later, he had settled back down enough for me to finish. I told him how Erin was so good, so trusting of me, and she went off to hide on my orders, not on her own. I told him about watching the explosion bellow out of the building as I fell to the ground, and the feeling of helplessness I had when I realized that she was somewhere in that fireball. I was so into the telling the story that I didn't notice I had started crying, as my grandfather now was.

After we regained our composure, Granddaddy had his hospital bed sit him up, so he was looking me in the eyes. The dark circles that ran beneath his eyes were like rings on a tree, not only giving away his age, but showing the marks that events had left on him. Looking into those eyes, I got to the hardest part of my tale, and began to tell him how Erin was haunting me; how I saw her and heard her almost everywhere I went, waking or dreaming. Granddaddy listened, nodding gently and taking in every detail.

When I was done, he asked, "Ellie, how old were you when I first took you out with me to take pictures?"

"Three or four. Why?"

Granddaddy shifted his weight and got a little closer, holding his hands out to me, each one in an L shape, then placing the points together to make a frame. It was just like when I was little, only his hands shook now, and I couldn't sit on his shoulders anymore.

"Do you remember what I said about framing the shot, my love?"

I reached back in my memory, but that was dozens of years ago, and literally hundreds of lessons later. "Not that day, no sir."

Granddaddy patted the bed at his side, so I could come sit beside him, and look through his makeshift frame with him. He'd gotten frail since Mama Jerri died, but there was still a strength in his presence that put me immediately at ease. While I was with my grandfather, nothing could touch me.

"Now, you look through the frame - that's your shot, right?" He asked. I nodded an affirmative as he continued. "OK then. That's your shot, but that's not your world, love. There are other shots to take after this one." The voice of four year old Ellie flowed from the recesses of my memory, matching my own as I asked, "Then what do you do, Granddaddy? How do you know which shot to take?"

197

My grandfather smiled. "Love, when you look through the eyepiece, you close one eye, to get a good idea of what you are getting. You want to see what you are missing, all you have to do is open the other eye."

It had been a hard technique to master as a child, but by the age of nine, I could frame up one shot and see my next, just by briefly opening both eyes as I snapped the shutter. Now, at twenty-eight, having both eyes open meant something totally different, and he knew it.

"Talk to Olivia about her sister, Ellie. You owe it to her, and you owe it to yourself," he said, his arms tiring of holding up the frame. "And most importantly, you owe it to Erin to not forget her. Not ever."

I stayed with Granddaddy for another hour before his afternoon meds knocked him out for a while. Walking out to my car, I noticed the honeysuckles were blooming, and likely had been since my return home. The sweet fragrance danced under my nose, then ever so gently it dashed away to find its next target. For the first time since I had been home, I felt like I was going to be all right. And if I was all right, I would do my damndest to make sure Olivia was too.

19
❧Appearance☙

Olivia sat quietly at the breakfast table, her stuffed rabbit placed on the table next to a bowl of cereal. She slowly picked through each of the coloured pieces of round puffed wheat, picking out each of the purple ones and setting them beside her bowl on the placemat, making a gross mix of soggy cereal and milk that grew with each minute.

"Olivia, honey," I said, reaching over to wipe up the milk before it found its way to the old rabbit or the floor. She stopped as I drew near, putting down her spoon and looking up at me with sad, blank eyes.

"Mama, I miss Erin," the small girl said quietly, the words barely forming on her ruby red lips. "Chester misses Erin too," she added, grabbing the rabbit and lowering his head solemnly, then picking him up in a close snuggle.

"I miss Erin too, honey. You know I'd do anything to bring her back," I answered, feeling a huge knot grow in my throat. I reached out to Olivia as I sat down at the table with her, and pulled her into my lap to hold her close. "I'd give my own life if it would bring her back, my love." Olivia sat up in my lap, and held Chester out to me. The old shaggy rabbit was clean now, and Forrest had bought new clothes for our favorite stuffy, but there would always be a worn look about him that told of his time in the Zone in Miami; I held Chester in my hand and wondered how a simple toy bunny could hold such a story in his eyes, and tell it so completely with his almost elderly appearance and the slight musty smell that would never quite wash away.

"Nana is coming by today, love." I said, trying to move the subject to a less overwhelming topic. "She and Aunt Chele are going to take you out for the day."

"Can Chester come with me, Mama?"

"Sure can, honey. Now Nana will be here in just a little bit. You gonna finish your cereal?"

Olivia got down and moved back to her seat, picking up her spoon and starting to fish through her meal again. "Yes, ma'am. I jus' gotta get the purple ones out first".

"Why the purple ones, love?" I asked, placing Chester on the edge of the table and moving to kneel beside my adopted daughter.

"They were Erin's favorite; but they hurt my tummy now. So I try and save them for her."

There are moments that I look back on my own childhood, and realize that my mom and my grandparents were much stronger than I ever knew. Looking down at this small girl remove the last of the purple cereal from her bowl, it took every ounce of willpower I had to not simply break down into tears all over again. I leaned over to kiss her on the head, and turned to walk into my kitchen, so I could find some way to let the tears flow just a little before they got the best of me. There was no way to know how many secret tears my own mother had cried for me during my childhood; if I asked her now, all she would say is, *'Oh love, I just did the best I could.'* I reached up to put plates from the washer back into my cupboard, and covertly wiped the growing pool of tears from my eyes. The last thing my little girl needed was to see me break down.

The front door chime brought me out of my daze and back to the moment. "Sweetheart, I think Nana's here!" I called to Olivia. I walked back into the dining room to see her take a huge spoonful of cereal and cram it into her mouth so she could finish up, and I found myself almost laughing as I remembered that I used to do the same thing when I was four. The front door sounded again, insisting that I answer its call. Imagine my surprise when I opened the front door to see not my mother, but my boss Director Forrest standing there.

"Jim! Hi there! It's so good to see you," I said as I gestured for him to enter. "I hadn't expected to meet with you till Monday, sir. Is everything alright?"

Jim Forrest smiled as he walked into my foyer, pausing to give me a small hug before continuing into the living room. "Oh, everything's fine Ellie. Your boys are ready to see you back at work, and we have a few cases requiring your expertise come Monday morning." I had rarely seen Jim in anything other than a nice suit, but you could clearly see he was here in an unofficial capacity. His Saturday morning wardrobe of Hawaiian shirts and Bermuda shorts would have served him well in Miami. Olivia came running up to him, calling, "JJ!"

as she opened her arms and nearly jumped up into his waiting embrace. Olivia held Forrest tight for a moment, then sat up in his arms and held out her rabbit to him as well. "Chester needs hugs too." She laughed when Jim gave Chester the rabbit a melodramatic, overly gratuitous hug before handing him back to Olivia.

"Liv, my dear. I need to talk to your mother in private for a bit. Will you be OK if Ellie and I go into the study?"

"OK. Bye bye JJ!" Olivia replied, blowing me a quick kiss and skipping back into the dining room to search for more breakfast cereal.

Jim and I went into my nearby study and pulled the door to, leaving it slightly open so I could listen out for Olivia. "What's up, boss?" I asked, taking a seat on the settee and offering a wingchair to Forrest. He pulled out a palm-sized reader out of his top pocket, and passed it over to me.

"The whole Miami underground is either on the run, or gunning for you, Ellyandra." Forrest said as I looked over the digital reports he'd handed me. "Their turf war has spread into Zones all across the country, including reports of some incitements here in Mobile." I skimmed the reports for more info and found that the faction formerly headed by Grummold had broken down into what could best be described as a civil war, slaughtering themselves, the Reeferistas, Listillios, and anyone who came in their path. Many of the remaining crime families were either leaving the Miami Dark Zone altogether, or looking for a way to get my head on a platter for helping ruin their perfect little haven.

"I kinda expected this. That's one of the reasons I took three months off." I said as I continued to shuffle through the reports, scanning each one quickly for a sign that it was noteworthy. "Don't tell me I'm being reassigned because of this."

"No, Ellie. But my superiors and I wanted to make sure that before you put yourself in harm's way on a daily basis that you knew what you were up against; especially now that you have a family to consider."

Jim continued to talk, but my eyes were scanning a report of another auction in Miami. It was a sideline - the report had nothing to do with me specifically, and was most likely downloaded to this reader as part of a batch. Forrest's words crept to the background as I read, "*Living doll, aged four years, for all your pleasures!*" The face on the hellish advertisement was one of an angel; large eyes and round, healthy cheeks, framed by ribbons of curls. It was a face I knew well; I had seen its likeness every day for months now.

I got up from my seat, moving towards my desk and activating my comm terminal. Jim stopped his speech, asking, "Ellie? Ellie, are you listening to me?"

"No, I'm not Jim. Sorry." I reached over and hit my auto dialer codes three and four, and soon had both Michaels and Zimmerman on my screen. "Boys, I need you. Can you meet me at the office, STAT?"

They both nodded in immediate agreement, and the screens went blank. Jim Forrest sat at an odd angle in his seat. "Ellie, what is going on?" He asked, trying to regain my attention.

"Reauthorize me today, Jim." I demanded, grabbing together my gear from the cabinet drawers in my study. "Today, right now, please. And my mother is coming to take Olivia for the day. Tell her it's going to be for a few days".

Forrest stood and began following me around the room as I put together a field kit for a trip to the Zone. "Fine, Ellie; but first you have to tell me what you are up to? Why this sudden drive to get back to work? What did you...?"

I handed the reader back to Jim, and pointed to the face on the screen. His eyes grew wide and he returned to his seat to let out a deep breath. Jim sat for a few moments, lost in his own thoughts, then finally responded. "OK, you are officially reauthorized and duly deputized as a Federal Agent again." He tapped some commands into his pocket computer, and held it out for me to thumbprint acknowledge, which I did as I walked past him to grab another package off my desk. "I'm marking your commission and all clearances fully reinstated as of now."

"Thank you Jim. Now if you will excuse me, I need to tell Olivia goodbye, then go meet with Michaels and Zimmerman. We have a job to do."

"Ellie," Jim called out, holding the reader in his hand and pointing out Erin's face on the ad. "Just what do you plan to do about this?"

"I'll worry about the details on the way there." I answered, sounding more abrupt with my boss than I should. "All you need to know is that I am going to get my daughter back."

20
❧Geronimo❧

Michaels and I hopped a cargo plane to Miami; it was the first plane leaving Mobile once we had a plan together, and the pilot was a friend of mine from school, so we were allowed to squeeze in between the crates of citronella candles headed to southern Florida. Three hours later, as our wheels touched down in Miami, I knew three things: I'd never travel this way again as long as I lived, and no mosquito for a hundred miles was likely to even come near me for months. I also knew I'd do it all over again if it meant my daughter's safe return to me.

Agent Gallindo was waiting for us outside. He stood in the drizzle holding the backdoor to a black SUV open for Michaels and I to enter. As much as I still blamed him for allowing my girls to be taken, I knew that his ineptitude did not mean he was untrustworthy. He was one of the few in Miami that still upheld the old code of 'protect and serve', and had never proven to be anything less than completely honest with me. And, if I was wrong, this would be the shortest mission of my career.

"Did you hear about the local excitement for the week, Ellie?"Gallindo asked as he drove us away from the airport, and towards the Federal Building in New Miami. "Someone piloted an old Soviet submarine into Biscayne Bay, and now the navy has them blockaded. We've had a standoff with an old Nuclear Sub going on for days now!"

Michaels and I both shrugged nonchalantly, each wondering if it was the same sub that had dumped us out in the waters four months ago.

"You think?" Michaels asked, smiling.

"Nah; couldn't be." I answered with a large grin. "Besides, those old things are a dime a dozen. No way it's the same one."

"One thing is for sure Ellie," Gallindo piped in, totally missing our moment. "Access to the Zone by water is right out. With all the raids from the zone, DC still has all access locked down."

I raised my eyebrow. "Raids? What do you mean raids?"

Gallindo spoke out to the vehicle. "Steve - take over please. Destination is Miami Federal; use the priority lanes if you have to." The vehicle responded with the traditional series of beeps and Gallindo's driver's seat turned around to face us.

"Pretty much anything you can imagine Ellie." His face twisted with a frown as he spoke. "Kidnappings, gang violence, targeted murders - the works. Bad thing is, we don't know how they are getting in and out. All the systems show that the security perimeter around New Miami hasn't been breached, but," he paused, hitting a few controls on the console and sending a hologram in front of us for Michaels and I to review. "Our intel shows that the crime bosses and cartel overlords are building an army to make a stand. Ever since they added light to their endeavors down there, they've sped up arming everyone in the Zone. They've got a small army now. We think the raids are just tests; simple one-off training missions, getting them ready for the big event."

"What's the big event?" Aaron asked, studying the hologram floating in the air between himself and Gallindo.

"Simple; they want it all for themselves. New Miami, the suburbs, and the outskirts. Except for New Miami, all buildings around the zone have been evaced. Director Cano ordered a one-mile buffer zone, and it's as desolate as they come. Of course, New Miami is still packed to the nines, and people can come and go - but all of us that stay are basically being held hostage by the cartels. They close down the Safeway, and we're stuck. No bones about it - we're screwed if they decide so."

"Why do you think they're holding you all hostage?" I inquired. "Nothing in this report says anything about that."

"We got a message the other day. Cartel leader named Diarzano sending us pictures of shaped explosives strapped into the supports for one of the platforms. Unless we get them safe passage in and out, and guarantee it stays that way, they're gonna bring down one of the sections of the New city."

I let my head drop back on the headrest of the backseat, thinking about the tens of thousands of people that would lose their lives if the gangs were

210

really stupid enough to bring any part of New Miami crashing down.

Gallindo continued. "Good thing is, Director Cano has a good head on his shoulders. He's the one that ordered the buffer zone, and he even keeps us out of there, so we don't get all shot up, or cause any problems while the negotiations are going on". Nothing in Gallindo's voice set the hair on my neck on end, but something about 'what' he said had me squirming on the inside.

"Did Cano say that?" I asked Gallindo, trying to keep my surprise in check. "I'd think he'd rely heavily on his people?"

"Oh, he has his special team, and they go in with him, but I'm not on that squad." Gallindo's tone became slightly sullen as he said this, turning around to take control of the vehicle again. He then perked up and added, "But when Cano is out in the field, I am in charge! So I do get to do some good."

We reached Miami Federal and Gallindo let us out at the front door. A quick flash of badges and retinal scans got us inside, but I didn't wait for Gallindo to return. I grabbed Aaron by the wrist, and remembering the surveillance system we'd encountered months ago, led him to the one place I felt we wouldn't be watched.

"Never been in a ladies room before Ellie." Michaels said as we hit the door. "Well, once in kindergarten, I tried to sneak in, but my teacher caught me - so that doesn't really count. Does it?"

"Why keep Federal Agents out of an evacuation Zone, Aaron?" I whispered as soon as the door closed behind us. "We know Director Cano has this building monitored thru and thru. He's also got prisoners that die mysteriously and people that just vanish on his watch. And now, Cano has everything locked out, with no agents except his hand-picked team allowed in the buffer zone, to 'keep the situation under control', but you and I know that is total BS. Washington would never allow that, and you know it".

"Special dispensation maybe? I don't know, Ellie." He sat down on a small bench in the ladies, then added, "…but it sure as hell is peculiar."

"Peculiar my ass." I paced around the small restroom, turning it over in my head, but only one thing made all the pieces fit.

"I think that Director Cano is in the back pocket of the cartels. Nothing else fits." Michaels started to protest, but I held up a palm so he'd let me continue. "Think about it; the Navy has the water blockaded, the Army has the land entrances blocked, and HQ says that no agents go in or out, but intel shows they are *growing* their army? Someone is letting people in. Isn't it convenient that Cano signed the order to create a buffer zone with no one there to watch, and doesn't let anyone but his own private team in or out? And that he goes in with them?"

Michaels was obviously disturbed at the thought, and began to toss out idea after idea - reason after reason - that Cano's orders could be legit. Each straw he grasped had a major problem, and try as he might, nothing else fit, unless Cano was on the payroll of the cartels.

"Ok then. What do we do?" he asked, looking dejected as he chose his words. "We still need to get in and grab Erin? How do we do that with no way in?"

"Easy," I responded, a sly grin breaking across my face. "We show a few cards here, make a few threats there, and cover our butts along the way. Go find Gallindo and let him know I need to meet with Director Cano. Then, get Zim. We're going to need his skills if we're going to pull this off."

****

My granddaddy had a saying that he took from an old movie. He used to smile as he received some honor or award, and say "*It's good to be the king*". While my grandfather had never let his achievements go to his head, the décor of Director Cano's Office announced the same could not be said for him. Lavish would not be a strong enough word to begin to describe the antique furnishings, modern art, and copious amounts of Gold and Platinum that lined even the most mundane items. I found myself feeling almost sick with the sheer pointlessness of it all as I stepped up and shook hands with a man I already didn't trust.

"Abyeto Cano" he said, extending his ring-clad hand out for a shake. "And you are Ellyandra Dyett. Damn fine work here. Turned a lot of heads". He sat after a brief handshake, and grabbed a cigar from a humidor on his desk. As he cut and lit the awful thing, he asked "So, what brings you back to Miami?"

There was no way I was going to tell him about Erin. "Well, Director" I said, taking a seat in front of the desk, "We've got intel that says you have a mole in your Division. D.C. wants me to take a look." I could hear Zim over my comm clicking speedily away, saying 'I hate it when you go off script Ellie!' Director Cano pulled up his comm, and nodded as he saw the 'orders' Zim had generated suddenly populate on his screen.

"What is it you really want, Agent?" he asked, puffing a ring of smoke into the air. "What evidence does HQ think they have of a mole here in Miami?"

I stood up and moved to sit on Cano's desk, crossing my legs and batting my eyes like I had when I was a little girl trying to con my grandfather out of candy. "Well, disappearing prisoners for one, secret surveillance lines for another, and the fact that you have so much disposable income that you can decorate this office like a cheap whorehouse doesn't help." I made sure to keep a huge, fake grin on my face as I said each line, reveling as Cano's cigar dropped into his lap.

I kept grinning, letting Cano stare at me for a minute or so. He finally asked, "OK - then I ask again, what is it *you* want, Agent?"

I leaned over Cano's desk, letting my bosom reveal just a hint of cleavage. "I need to get into the Zone."

"Why?"

"None of your business why, Abyeto. Just know that if you get me in, and allow safe passage out, then HQ doesn't have to know that I found a damn thing."

"You haven't found a thing, Agent." Cano picked up his cigar and relit it, blowing smoke right in my face. It took all I had to not reach out and knock the hell out of him. "But, if I let you in, you're likely gonna die anyway, so either way, I win. Meet me on the west access point at noon; Gate B3. We'll get you into the Zone."

****

Gate B3 was indeed on the west side of the Safeways that ringed New Miami. It had been a major highway half a century ago, but now was reduced to a few sliding concrete doors almost fifty feet high, and barbed wire/ electro wire fences that could rob the life of any healthy person. The surrounding area couldn't have looked any more like a post-apocalypse urban ruin film if it had a professional set decorator. Burned out husks of building, large pieces of fallen brick facade and more piles of rubbish and debris filled the area on both sides of the access point. It was vaguely reminiscent of Post World War II Germany. The shadow of New Miami painted itself straight down to the earth, telling me it was high noon.

A few silent minutes went by before we heard the hum of a transport, and one of the oversized square vehicles came up over the hill and stopped almost fifty feet away. At least sixty well-armed sniper troops exited, making a half circle in front of the vehicle. Cano stepped out of the front, and motioned for us to join them.

"I don't like this Ellie." Michaels said quietly his voice almost lost amid the crunch of gravel that each step created on the old roadway.

"Stick to the plan, Aaron."

We soon reached Director Cano and his team. The midday sun was blazing, and only now that we had come close to them could I see that these men were not carrying the standard Federal Issue Pulsers - they had guns. Big guns, and lots of them. Cano raised a hand when we were a good ten feet away, and each of those guns became trained on me and

Michaels. We raised our hands over our heads, but none of the guns lowered.

"Trying to sneak into the Zone despite the lockdown, I see." Cano announced so his men could hear. "My orders say I can shoot to kill." We were outnumbered by at least thirty to one, so even with my best acrobatics, there was no way I could avoid being hit if he gave the order to fire.

"What about our deal, Abyeto?" I asked, using his first name as an intentional sign of disrespect. Cano strode up and slapped me across the face, his men each re-aiming as I reacted to make sure that no retaliation was given.

The hot sun shone down on my head as I spoke, almost whispering "Why kill us? We're not the enemy?"

Cano laughed at me as he reached into his coat pocket for another cigar. "Not to the Bureau, no. But you are my enemy. The cartels have paid me well to clean up their dirty work, and as long as I have these idiots working on my side, I can keep raking up a big ol' pile of money."

"So it's about money? No political ideology? No spiritual path - just money?" I shot Michaels a look and a small nod. He nodded back, and placed his hand across his raised wrist.

"Yup - who needs God or politics when you have good old American Capitalism, and the all mighty credit," Cano answered smugly. Then, leaning in and whispering so only Ellie could hear, Cano added, "I don't even need these men. If they get in my way, I'll have them killed, too." He blew another puff of cigar smoke in my face, then turned to walk back to his troops.

His men were correcting their stance, getting ready to fire as soon as he was no longer in their path. I knew I wouldn't have another chance, so I took a deep breath and called out behind him, saying, "Before you have me shot to death, can I tell you one last thing? It's something I think you need to know."

Cano's footsteps stopped, and he turned to look at me with utter annoyance. "What could you possibly have to say to me?"

This was the moment we'd been waiting for, and Michaels hit a hidden control under his sleeve. Suddenly, our Mobile Robotic Crime Scene Analyzers started coming out of hiding. They came from around broken buildings and from behind signs and billboards that had fallen to the ground long ago.

They came from behind abandoned cars, and from up the road behind Cano's team. There were dozens of them, rolling towards the armed agents, and each one was playing back Cano's words, this time loud enough so his men could hear him.

"I don't even need these men. If they get in my way, I'll have them killed, too". His voice rang out loud and clear, and before any of the surprised men could respond, each of them had a MR-CSA parked right in front of them.

Cano's men all lowered their weapons, listening to their boss's words play over and over again. Cano himself stood in the middle of the road, his face turning bright red as he stared at me with hatred. After half a minute, a man in sergeant stripes stepped around his MR-CSA, and leveled his weapon at Cano, saying "Director Cano. Please drop your weapons and come with us."

Soon the other men were responding in kind, each one likely feeling used, astounded and ashamed of what they had been part of. Cano could see that his little reign was over, and with a battle cry rivaling a wounded banshee, Cano rushed at me, bridging the distance in a flash, and drew a gun on me. Before any of the other agents could intercept, I went into an attack on Cano, not only disarming him, but laying him flat on his back in one swoop.

By the time Cano's special team reached their disgraced boss, he was bloodied and out of breath, his expensive suit in disheveled tatters on his frame. Sergeant Tiermo handcuffed Cano and read him his rights. He was roughly brought to his feet, but before he was escorted away I couldn't help but enjoy one last jab.

"Hey Abyeto; if you're going to be a selfish bastard, don't ever admit it to anyone, especially to someone with a commlink in her ear."

Sergeant Tiermo passed the disgraced Director to his men, and approached me with his radio in hand. "Agent Dyett?" Tiermo was looking past me, and couldn't meet my eyes.

"It's Ellie. And you didn't know." Tiermo looked to the ground.

"Should have. Too many promises of too much."

"We don't have time for that now Sergeant. I need to get into the Zone and I need in now."

Sergeant Tiermo handed me his radio. "Agent Gallindo is asking for a follow up. Fill him in, and I'll get those doors open."

My conversation with Gallindo was short lived. Zim had already been in contact with Gallindo when he took control of Miami's entire team of MR-CSA's, and Washington had, at my bosses' insistence, issued orders giving me temporary oversight of the Miami Federal District while Michaels and I were en route to the Dark Zone gate. By the time I got to talk to Gallindo, it was all "Yes Ma'am" with no questions asked.

"Watch your back Gallindo," I added, after lining up some more muscle to be delivered to the Zone. "We don't know how many of these men may still be loyal to Cano. Be careful."

"What are you going to do now, "Director Dyett?" Gallindo asked. I could almost hear the smile on his face.

"I came here to stop something horrible; now, we're going to make sure its stopped for good."

21
~Carnage~

I had never entered the Miami Dark Zone without sneaking in. This was usually done by water, sewer, or passages so old that even the rats had forgotten about them. Now, I found myself walking down a deserted, broken highway, with desolation on every side, sunlight dwindling at my back, and an unnatural glow on the manmade ceiling ahead. Here on the outskirts, the shadows crouched in corners, waiting for us to pass, and we could only hope that these shadows didn't envelop people who would fight to kill us.

We usually went into the Zone with a small team - three to five agents at the most. Thanks to Cano bringing his special ops unit to the scene, and Zim's recruitment of a good forty MR-CSA's, I now felt like the lead scout of a small platoon.

"Zim," I asked, knowing that even though he was hundreds of miles away in Mobile, he was listening in on the comm in my ear and following our every move. "How did you coordinate this many MR-CSA's? Usually anything more than three, and they are running into each other like no one's business."

Zim's signal was starting to get a little scratchy. "I tied motion control of each into the helmet cams of your Special Ops team. They use that telemetry to see where they are going. The rest is pretty easy."

Leave it to Zim to think that coordinating forty robotic units would be easy. Of course, I'd played video games with him before, and often wondered if Zim wasn't hard lined into a server somehow. He could do things with Virtual Reality that the programmers never planned for, and more than once he'd brought down a simulation with his 'creative' way of dealing with anything computer based.

The main road in was fairly open for the first few hundred feet, and it was obvious that people and vehicles had been moving through the area on a regular basis. Debris had been moved to the side of the asphalt, and fresh tire tracks left their overlapping trails in the dirt. Several sets of tracks led to side streets that were mostly either closed off, or blocked with vehicles to bar easy entry.

"Ellie," Michaels said quietly."Looks like the road ends ahead; some sort of barricade." Michaels took control of one of the MR-CSA's on his handheld, and swung it ahead of our group to go get a look. The barricade was only a good fifty feet away, but the artificial sunlight over the center of the zone provided a hideous backlight that made night vision useless, and details non-existent.

"Oh my God, Ellie!" Michaels said, stopping dead in his tracks. "The MR-CSA just scanned the barricade."

"And? What is it? A bomb? A trap?" I didn't give him time to answer, I just took the handheld from him and looked for myself. The MR-CSA scan showed rebar and concrete - and bodies. Dozens of bodies, all impaled on the protruding rebar and stacked up to make a blockade. Sergeant Tiermo stood behind me, looking at the image of the macabre device that blocked our way. He reached into his shirt and pulled out a Rosary, and started a quiet "My Father".

I turned around, giving the handheld back to Michaels, and faced the group that had been ordered to kill me less than an hour ago. "OK. Here's the deal, Gentlemen. The people we are dealing with - the ones that had your former boss in their back pocket - are not just murderers. They are sick, twisted bastards who killed a bunch of people just to make a fence. And as sad as that is, as frightening as that may be, we can't let it stop us. We have to keep going."

****

It took us at least fifteen minutes to find a route around the blockade, and instinct told us all that we were being watched. Michaels had taken the lead with his map, and after more twists, turns, and dead ends than I cared to count, we finally made it into territory that I recognized. When I had lived under cover in the zone, the darkness made this place look less like Hell. Now, in the odd brown-blue glow of the spotlights that bounced off the platforms above, every scarred building, burnt-out home and abandoned vehicle looked like something from a horror movie.

Sergeant Tiermo spoke quietly as we moved. "Director Dyett, something's just not right. Every time I have been this far into the Zone, it's been crowded. Very crowded." He waved his hand around in front of his head, adding, "Where is everyone?"

Tiermo was right. While the outskirts of the Zone were always empty, most of the Miami Zone was packed to the nines. Aside from a few lost souls, stoned out of their minds and propped up against buildings or cars, there was no one. Michaels took his handheld out and used the nearest MR-CSA to do a quick scan or the surrounding area.

"Ellie, we are definitely not alone." He handed me the tiny computer and pointed to the images of the buildings around us. "Each red dot indicates a heartbeat, El." All the buildings around us were practically glowing red, showing they were teaming with people.

"Any way to tell if they are armed, Aaron?"

Michaels just gave me a look, then answered "Oh, how about all the weapons we saw them passing out like candy a few months ago? I'd be surprised if they weren't armed!"

Of course we'd had our suspicions about being watched since we entered the Zone. Unless everyone had voluntarily left, there was simply no way we wouldn't have run into hordes of people by now. Plus, I knew there was no way I could get a troop this size all the way to the auction site without being noticed. Now, it made sense that we'd made it

227

in this far with no resistance; they were waiting for us. It was a trap.

"Fall back, Tiermo. Slowly." Sergeant Tiermo opened his mouth to protest, but I cut him off, interjecting, "No time for a huddle, and no looking like we are planning. That's the surest way to let on that we know we're being watched. We can talk out our next step while looking like we are lost. That may buy us some time before they decide we've gone far enough."

There is a definite perk to being in charge, and even though my position here was temporary, I planned on using every advantage to get to Erin before it was too late. Michaels, Tiermo and I talked quietly as we pretended to reference the map, and made it look like we were completely turned around. While that wasn't actually far from the truth, I knew that eventually we'd find our way to our destination; the Zone was big, but it wasn't New York sized enormous. I had an idea on how to get to Erin, but neither of the boys seemed to agree. Even Zim, virtually sitting in my ear, was protesting over our hidden commlink, but none of them had a better idea.

"You cannot go off alone in this place Ellie!" Michaels said, almost letting his aggravation elevate his volume. "There is something big about to go down, and you need some protection if you are going to get to Erin."

Zimmerman chipped in, with a staticy "If you break away, and get taken out, it could be months before we even find you. You know the Caribbean faction in the Miami Zone has been accused of Cannibalism. We might never find you!"

Only Tiermo said nothing. He walked slowly at my side, listening to every word, and filling in Zim's commentary by my audible responses. After a few minutes of bickering, I turned to him and asked, "Ok, Sergeant. What's your take? You want to treat me like a Princess too, and keep me safe?"

Sergeant Tiermo stopped cold. He turned to look directly at Michaels and me, and spoke so quietly we almost couldn't hear him. "Ms. Dyett; Ellie." He paused to make sure the familiar use of my name was OK, then continued. "You lived in the Zone for a month earlier this year. If any of us would be alright on their own, it would be you." He then looked Michaels directly in the eyes, and added, "Plus, you are currently the Director here in Miami, are you not? It's not my place to question your orders, Ma'am. That being said, I do have a suggestion or two that might make this work out for everyone's concerns."

****

We split into three groups. Tiermo assigned his best, most stealthy men, to follow me at a distance. Zim of course had to ask how they had Ninja's in Miami, and we had none assigned to Mobile. They may not have been ninjas, but as soon as I headed off on my own, I sure as hell couldn't see them. Even in the twisted mix of sickly light and almost solid shadows, these men had vanished into the surroundings. I knew they had my back.

Team two, led by Sergeant Tiermo, made their way towards the building where the girls had been kept - towards the place where we thought Erin had died. He believed that, even thought part of it has been blown to hell, that building was some sort of headquarters. Michaels and I had explored little to none of the lower floors, save that which led to the girls. There could be people, information, or any number of useful things in that old place, and Tiermo was more than willing to take the risk, not only to redeem himself and his men, but to stop the criminal enterprises that had taken total control just a few hundred feet below New Miami.

Michaels took the remaining men and MR-CSA's back to the fence of impaled bodies we'd discovered earlier. Scans showed that was the border.

Buildings on the inside of the fence were packed tight with people. It was as good a marker as any, and gave us the advantage of a somewhat defensible exit. Now that my boys were in place, and we had a better plan for the situation, it was my turn. It was time to go get my girl.

****

22
❧Surprises❧

I had been in probably two dozen Dark Zones across the country over the last few years. All of them, no matter what region or climate, had a few things in common. There was the need for a light source, since the overhead platforms and roadways blocked out the sun. Urban ruin was another constant. Buildings in the Zones had been in disrepair for decades as the new cities were built. Despite this fact, most Zones were, if not packed full, at least sporadically filled with the poor, forgotten and lost of society. While the rest of us enjoyed the fruits of the despair and turmoil of the early twenty-first century, these people, thousands upon thousands of them, had been left out. And the Zones were the only place they had to go.

It was odd to not run into any people in the Zones, but even more so in Miami. Estimates put the DZ population here around thirty-three thousand. Most of that number was taken up with illegals, criminals and workers kept in line with guns and drugs, but, as warped as it was, there was a thriving economy in the Miami zone, and plenty of semi-willing hands ready to do the work. Making my way towards what had once been Grummold's auction house, these facts made the empty streets more ominous and threatening than they had been when filled past capacity. Equally disturbing was the silence. When I was under cover here, there was hardly a minute that the reverberation of machinery or the sound of gunfire didn't fill the air, bouncing off the concrete above. Now, the gunfire was absent, and the machines had seemingly been shut down. I could almost hear the hum of the giant spotlights that lit the ceiling above, setting the stifling air almost on fire with their heat.

I still couldn't see the men who were supposed to be following me, which either meant they had hauled off and ran when they had the chance, or they were very good at their jobs. Either way, I couldn't worry about it now; I was almost to my destination. Turning one last corner, I saw the ruinous place where I had met my daughters. The doors were opened wide, and light from inside danced and mingled with the glow from overhead. The place was, as expected, filled to capacity. I pulled away from the edge of the building I had been sneaking along, held a deep breath, and took the strides needed to take me inside.

Bidders were once again mulling about, and the front of the room held a small stage with a podium. Of course, Grummold was dead and gone. A large man in a black overcoat sat behind the podium, acting as auctioneer and Master of Ceremonies. His wisps of straggly white hair did their best to cover his balding head. The man's face was scarred from burns on one side, making his features almost as twisted as the Zone itself. Despite the scars and pulled taunt skin, he looked familiar. It was only when he turned his head to the other side that I could place him. It was Prospero - the man who had taken the girls from Miami Federal.

Prospero's' raspy voice rang out as he slammed the gavel down, announcing, "Round Six - bidding is up to 150,000 credits. Place your bets!" Two men sat at the bidding machine, going thru the same torturous shocks that I had endured months earlier, as bookies took handfuls of both cash and bidding sheets. After a minute, a bell rang, and

234

bidding stopped. The crowd fell silent as the juice started to pour through the bidders, adding a tinge of ozone to the smell of musk and body odor that permeated the room. Soon, the penetrating smell of burning flesh cut through the mix, and the bidder on the left fell to the ground, burned, bleeding and unconscious. The silent crowd was suddenly in an uproar, with shouts of victory and curses for the defeated filling the room.

Amid all the hubbub, I took advantage of the spectacle to sneak behind the crowd, and around to the corner of the stage to take a look at the goods. There, under a blanket, hooked up to a small IV pump, was Erin. Her breath was shallow, and her eyes rolled and lolled about in her head, telling me instantly that she was drugged. On her face were no signs of burns, or any other damage from the explosion. Of course, I wondered how she had gotten away in the first place.

I started to reach out to touch Erin's face, and silence abruptly took the room. I was so close to my little girl, but I couldn't get to her. Not yet.

Prospero looked over to me, holding up his hand to still the bidders and guards in the room who were ready to jump me. "I know you, little girl." He motioned a quick signal, and I found myself whisked into the arms of two guards, and placed within inches of the podium. Prospero leaned down, getting close enough for me to see the lines of burned flesh and ridges of scar tissue in all their grotesque detail. "Yes, I know you. You are the little bitch who blew up my property." He snarled as he sat back, narrowing his eyes in a hateful expression. "If not for you, I'd not have these scars." He placed his fingertips together and rested his elbows on his enormous stomach, looking deep in thought. Finally, after a moment he continued. "Perhaps an eye for an eye, or in this case, a face for a face, would be a fair trade."

One of his men drew a switchblade from their side, extending the razor sharp metal with the flip of their wrist, and started toward me. "You don't want to do that, Prospero. Not unless you want to blow this place up, too."

Prospero raised his hand again, stopping his hooligan with a gesture. "So you know my name. Cute. Now tell me, just how do you plan on blowing up this facility? And why would you, considering I know you've come to save the girl - not kill her."

The room was silent, each set of ears waiting for my answer. Oddly, it reminded me of my second grade Christmas Play. I was a snowflake, and all the other kids were after me. I only had one line, and I was deathly afraid of screwing it up. Needless to say, my nerves got the better of me, I screwed up my line, and the whole troupe was angry with me till February. By the time my third grade Christmas Play came around, I had worked hard to make sure I had control over my stage fright. Back then, all that was at risk was my social life. Now, in this place, surrounded by the worst of humanity, my continued existence depended on my acting.

"Before I came after her, I took a page from Grummold's book." Breaking an arm free of the men holding me in place, I reached up to my armourweave, and unhooked the front panel, then pulled aside part of my shirt, revealing a scar over my left breast. I narrowed my eyes at him, asking coolly, "I think you call it 'Spite', isn't that right?"

Prospero's eyes widened, anger flaring his nostrils when he made the connection. "You wouldn't! It isn't possible!" Prospero grabbed a device from under the podium and held it up to me. I could feel a beam of energy and a pulse of sound envelop my torso as he scanned me, trying desperately to uncover my deception. Fortunately for me, Zim had anticipated this when we came up with this fabrication, and he'd placed a tiny patch just underneath my skin that, if scanned, would give a false signal and show up as an explosive hooked up like a pacemaker. We'd tested it with equipment both old and new before we left Mobile, and each time Zim's false image showed up the same. Now, I was holding my breath, in hopes that it wouldn't fail me here.

I knew Zim's magic had worked when Prospero yelled in hatred, and threw the scanner across the room. "I'll kill you later, child!" He turned his attention to the guards on either side of me, nearly spitting out their names in his rage. "Reaton! Malen! Tie her up in the corner!"

****

I had no delusions about this mission. I knew there was no way I'd just be able to waltz in, grab Erin, and head home; it just didn't work like that, and I knew it. So when Prospero's men tied me up in the back corner and bidding continued, it worked to my advantage. It wasn't long before all eyes were glued to the new men bidding for my daughter. It reminded me of cock fighting, only with humans. Each of these men were torturing the other, and the people gathered round couldn't get enough of the blood and gore. Seeing this spectacle, I found myself grateful that Erin was unaware of what was going on around her.

Being involved in this once was more than anyone deserved; twice was unthinkable.

The room was awash with hoots, hollers and screams as the next round took hold. Using this to my advantage, I slipped my fingers into the sleeve of my left arm, and pulled on a tiny hook that was built into the cuff. This released microscopic nanites that were programmed to be attracted to, and to consume, any type of binding. These little guys would eat through rope, nylon, twine, duct tape, and even zip ties. It was only a few minutes before I could pull my hands apart, and the rope binding my wrists virtually dissolved. I took great care when I broke my bonds that I didn't draw attention to myself. After a few test movements proved that no one was paying any attention to me, I slowly moved away from the back corner of the room, and headed toward the door. If I could get back outside, maybe I could get a couple of MR-CSA's to help me with a diversion. Or maybe I could meet up with the other teams and storm the gates, so to speak. I was considering every option I could think of as I rounded the edge of the doorway, and ran right into a man who'd just arrived. He was tall, with broad shoulders, and an old style military uniform that squared his form. The man reached out and grabbed me by the arms, cautiously looking me over as his men formed a blockade behind him. He passed me to one of his men, saying in a thick Slavic accent, "Our business is done. I have no need of you."

The current round of bidding ended with a huge surge of electricity that caused the lights to flicker, and brought one of the bidders to his death. Prospero motioned for the body to be removed, and looked up to see the Submarine Captain approaching him. He also noticed me in the custody of the old Pirates crew.

"Captain Vladislav, to what do I owe the honor?" Prospero half stood to reach out a hand to the Captain. "I understand your vessle is stuck in our little harbor. Perhaps you need a way out?"

Half the crowd was leaving now, pushing out past us since the bidding had gotten 'too rich for their blood.' Only a handful of bidders remained, but Captain Vladislav's men took up most of the space the now absent bidders had vacated. Vladislav signaled one of his crew to the front, and the man stepped up alongside his master, obediently depositing a large sack on the podium.

The Captain returned the handshake. "I have no need for your assistance in leaving this place, though the offer is appreciated." His thick accent was as prevalent now as it had been the night he helped Michaels and me sneak into the Zone. "However," he continued, "I am somewhat interested in the merchandise you have for sale today." With this, Captain Vladislav untied the sack, and reached in to pull out a handful of gold coins. "Smuggling has its advantages, yes?"

"It would seem so!" Prospero answered, holding out his hand as the Captain let a few of the coins drop over Prospero's fingers and back into the sack. "How much is here?"

"In your credits, five million." Captain Vladislav tied the end of the sack, and handed it back to his yeoman. "Of course, in trade markets elsewhere, it could be more, or less."

Prospero's greedy eyes lit up hungrily as he reached out for the sack of coins. The lone bidder who had survived the last round stood up, protesting "Hey, what about my bid?"

Prospero seemed almost shocked when the bedraggled man spoke, almost as though he'd forgotten anyone else was present. He slowly turned his head to the man, and asked, "Can you top five million?" The man sat, looking as though he were doing math in his head, then finally answered, "No; I don't think I can go that high." Before he could say another word, Prospero pulled a gun from his overcoat, and placed the hand cannon to the man's head. For just a moment, he looked as though he was going to say something, perhaps even let the man go. Then without warning, the trigger was pulled and the target's cranium was obliterated. Prospero immediately turned his attention back to the Captain and his gold.

Vladislav reopened the sack of coins, placing it back on the podium. He then walked over to Erin, who was still laying on the small stage, mostly obscured by her blanket. Vladislav pulled the blanket away and saw the IV pump that was keeping her medicated.

"How long has she been this way?" the captain asked. Prospero could hardly acknowledge the man, such was his obsession in his gold. Vladislav roughly cleared his throat, and asked again. "Prospero. How long has she been drugged?"

"Eh?" Prospero responded, half in his dream world of money, and half pulled back to earth with the rest of us. "Oh - since the explosion...so several months now. I wanted to make sure she didn't try and get away, especially after being hurt protecting her from the explosion."

I couldn't help but respond to this. "Why would *you* protect her?" I bit back my urge to curse the man. It was like Prospero had almost forgotten I was there as well. He turned his attention to me.

"Oh. Well, it's really a matter of investment." Prospero got down from the stool that he'd used behind the podium, and walked over to me. He got right in my face, then answered, "Ugly little girls only sell for half the price." Prospero then reached into his overcoat, only now realizing he'd not put his weapon back in its holster. The gun was still on the podium, several steps away.

No sooner than he'd turned to walk back and grab the device he would use to rob me of my life, the doors behind us burst open. My Special Forces team flooded the hall, each with large weapons they quickly trained on Prospero's men and the Captain's crew. I breathed a sigh of relief until I saw Tiermo enter. He was carrying something large on his shoulders. Sergeant Tiermo walked right up to the stage and threw his bundle - an unconscious Michaels - hard to the floor.

"Do you really think my allegiances would switch so easily, Ellie?" Tiermo asked. He walked over to Prospero, and bent down to kiss his ring.

Prospero gently patted Tiermo's head as he did so, then gestured for him to stand.

"I take it Cano is dead?" Prospero asked.

Tiermo nodded an affirmative, then added, "At least, he will be by the time he reaches Miami Federal."

Prospero turned his attention back to Captain Vladislav. "The drugs we selected to keep her will have no lasting effects. If we unplugged her now, she'd be awake within the hour, none the worse for her wear."

"Then unplug her," Captain Vladislav commanded. "I may want to begin as soon as we get back to my ship. Once I am done, my men may have her as well."

Prospero stepped up onto the stage, talking aloud as he disabled the pump. "Code 272, release." The tiny device shut down, and Prospero removed the IV in Erin's arm. "As far as she'll remember, it's just lost time. She will have no memory of recent events, and we have made sure she is unsoiled." Prospero's promise that Erin had not been sexually abused while in his company made me hate him no less, but it was still good to hear.

'Frame it up, Ellie'. I could almost hear my granddaddy's' voice in the back of my mind. I was about to miss something if I wasn't careful.

'Look at your shot, hon.' I looked around carefully, taking note of each person's position and distance from one another. Tiermo was closest to me on the right, and I could see not only his bayonet sticking up from his armourweave, but if I timed my move just right, I could see myself getting his rifle as well. There was a crewman to my left and slightly behind me, then the bulk of the rest behind him.

'No time like the present, Granddaddy.' I said to myself, taking a deep breath and spinning to my left, grabbing the arm of a guard and swinging him back into the others. I used his momentum to fling myself towards Tiermo, and grabbed his bayonet with one hand, twisting around him to place the blade at his neck, then reaching back around him with my right arm and grabbing his rifle butt. Between the Special Forces, Captain Vladislav's crew, and Prospero's guards, there had to be sixty if not seventy people who suddenly had weapons trained on me, and Tiermo was my only shield. Tiermo, and the idea that if they killed me, I'd blow up and take them all to hell with me.

245

"Don't shoot her!" Prospero warned the new arrivals. "She's been implanted with explosives. She'll kill us all if we kill her!"

"Put 'em down!" I commanded to the room. Captain Vladislav, Prospero and Tiermo all nodded, and slowly their men each dropped their weapons to the floor. "Now," I said, pushing Tiermo away towards his men, and turning his rifle on myself, "It's time to play a little game. We can either play nice, and no one gets hurt, or any one of you primates who wants to risk being a hero can cause us all to be blown to teeny, tiny bits. I guarantee you I can pull this trigger and stop my own life faster than any of you idiots could even come up with a plan more complex than running away like children."

I walked over to the podium and grabbed Prospero's gun, placing the huge caliber barrel under my chin. "Anyone want to say I'm wrong? Time to place your bets, Gentlemen."

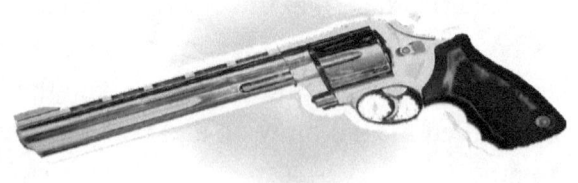

23
❧Bidding❧

It is truly amazing what people will do when they think you are a walking bomb. It also helps when they think you are more than just a bit 'touched' as my Granddaddy used to say. Tiermo's men were the most cooperative, not only gathering the weapons of the others, but helping tie up not only Prospero's guards, but Vladislav's men and each other as well. Of course, that left me to tie up Tiermo, so I knocked the traitor out cold with the butt of his own rifle before tying him up. I also made sure that none of the Special Forces crew had the nanites I'd used to free myself earlier. I had the upper hand for the moment, and I was damned determined to keep it.

Eventually, Michaels started to wake, sporting a shiner that had his left eye swollen shut, bruises and cuts galore, but overall none the worse for wear. Once we had the place secure, I ran over to Erin, who was starting to rouse slightly. Like waking from a bad dream, she slowly opened her eyes and saw my face. A muffled 'Ellie' is all that came out before she closed her eyes again, still mostly asleep from the drugs that had too long kept her under.

I pulled away the blanket, and scooped Erin into my arms, getting ready to carry her out of this little piece of hell and away to safety, when Prospero spoke. "Agent, are you aware of all the uses in Medicine for Carbon Nanotubes?" There was an air of superiority in his voice that went right through me. I stopped, holding Erin toward Michaels, then turned back to see Prospero getting to his feet.

"You see," he continued, steadying himself against the podium, his hands still bound behind his back, "For thirty years now, the technology has existed, even been improved upon. Certain cancers can be cured with a simple injection of Carbon Nanotubes, each filled with a strong chemical agent that targets cancer cells and destroys them, leaving healthy cells perfectly fine."

"What are you talking about?" I asked, anger and annoyance just barely contained in my response. "I know all about Carbon Nanotubes."

"Well, maybe not *everything*, Agent. For example, you don't know what *I've* done with them." Prospero smiled what could only be called a wicked, evil smile followed with a small laugh that was uncharacteristically shrill for a man his size. "If I were you, I wouldn't take her out of that door; not unless you want to watch her die a horrible, painful death."

I gently placed Erin next to Michaels in one of the open seats, bending over to kiss her forehead. Then I turned, slowly, and stepped over to the podium, fury bubbling up inside me. We were so close! Almost able to leave, and now this fat bastard had done something else to my child! I picked up the solid wood podium, and tossed it across the room into the far wall, and watched it shatter into splinters and pieces as I let out a howl. After a moment, I straightened my armourweave, stood back up straight, and walked back to Prospero, not getting too close, but close enough to get my point across.

I said in a low, quiet voice, "Alright then. What now?" I glared at the man with as much anger as I could muster without losing control. I wanted him to feel threatened, and after my little display, he sure as hell should have.

"Well, little girl, it's like this." Prospero moved to sit on the edge of the stage, next to the bidding machine that had already taken several lives today. "I am willing to make a deal with you. I'll give you the trigger device, and you can take the merchandise and have all the Nanotubes filtered out of her blood. Of course, if she gets too far away from the trigger, she's as good as dead, but that would be your problem."

"Why don't I just kill you now, and take the device with me?" I asked tersely.

"Because, you don't know where it is, or what it looks like. And you won't take that chance, now will you?" I hated to admit it, but Prospero was obviously a good chest player, and had planned out many moves in advance, anticipating dozens of permutations in the game.

"What is the catch?" I asked. "There is no way you are just going to let me walk out of here with Erin."

"You have to earn her first." Prospero answered, nodding his head towards the bidding machine. "You against the Captain; winner takes all. If you win, you and your friend walk away with the child. If he wins, I not only get my five million in gold, but we get to sell you and your man over there."

"How can you risk that without blowing us all up?" I asked, not forgetting that I was supposed to be chock full of explosives that would go off if I died.

"Because the scan is a lie. You'd never implant real explosives in yourself, because it would be too risky for the child. Even if you died, you'd hope your friend over there would still be able to get her to safety. "

There was no need to deny it now. All the other men were bound and couldn't act to harm me now. "When did you figure that out?" I asked, curious as to where my act had failed.

"It took me a bit," Prospero replied, "but after your friend woke I heard you two talking. You let slip that someone named Zimmerman did a good job with the implant. He asked if it worked, and you said like a charm. That implies it has already done its job, and since you haven't blown us all up, I can only imagine its job is something less violent. Something like subterfuge."

I looked over to Michaels, sitting with his arm around a girl I thought had been dead for months.

The very notion of risking her life on the chance that Prospero was lying now was just too great a chance to take. I walked over to them, and knelt at Erin's side, gently pushing her curls away to look at her sweet face.

"Aaron, do you have anything on your Comm?" I asked. Mine had been oddly silent since I had entered the Auction Hall.

"Not even static, El." Michaels answered.

"I have to do this Aaron." He'd been listening to our conversation, though he could hardly see much through his swollen eye. "But if this goes wrong, you have to find a way to save her. Either that, or ..."

Michaels put his hand over my mouth, stopping me mid thought. "Nope. We're not going there, Ellie." He lowered his hand and added, "Besides, I saw the scans from your last time in the bidding machine. You're gonna kick that guys ass!"

I tried to manage a smile for my friend, then leaned over to snuggle my girl for what could be the last time. Considering we had all believed her life had ended months ago, I considered each additional second a gift. No matter how this turns out, I was lucky.

"Ok, Prospero." I announced, standing, Then, I walked over to Captain Vladislav. "I'm game. What about you, Admiral?"

"There is no need to provoke me." Vladislav's voice was level, with no consternation or emotion. "I will have the girl, and perhaps I will even have you, if I feel like a bit of Necrophilia. You will not survive this encounter."

I walked back over to Michaels and gave him one of the rifles we'd taken from Tiermo's men.

"I'm going to untie them now Aaron." Looking at the two men over my shoulder, I added, "If either one tries anything we haven't discussed already, shoot them both."

"Yes, Ma'am!" Michaels replied. Even with one eye out of commission, in these close quarters, Michaels was a crack shot. I knew he had my back.

****

The bidding machine looked different than it had all those months ago. There were still straps to hold ones hands in place, but now there was also a dial next to the right hand, and five switches next to the left. They were positioned in such a way that you could manipulate them even with your hands tied down to the flat top of the device. Of course, metal plates were also part of the design, and once strapped into the machine, there was simply no avoiding the points of contact.

Prospero strapped Captain Vladislav in first, then moved over to me. As he took my left wrist and placed it against the metal plate, I looked up at him and said, "I swear to God, if this isn't fair, or you have this rigged, Michaels will shoot you in the head before you can bat an eyelash."

Prospero tightened the strap, and moved to the right hand, not saying a word, simply smiling quietly to himself. He strapped my right hand in place, and stepped away, leaning in to flip a switch on the base of the unit. We could all hear the machine hum to life, and the smell of electricity overtook my senses in moments. Prospero straightened himself up, and looked down over the Captain and me.

"The rules are simple. At your right hand, you see a dial. It controls voltage and amperage, depending on which switches you have selected at your left hand. You turn the dial to increase or decrease, and flip the switches to try and out maneuver your opponent."

"Is there a reason I should not simply turn the dial up all the way and finish this now?" Captain Vladislav inquired, his fingers gingerly caressing the dial on his side of the table.

"Excellent question. You see, the circuits inside are always in motion; turning up the dial can increase the current going through your opponent, but the higher you go, the stronger the shocks you will also receive. Plus, some of the switches change the frequency of the current. This can cause a relatively small current to do massive damage to muscles and skin, and oscillating the frequency can do permanent nerve damage. The trick is to figure out the best combination of switches and dial settings to take out your opponent before they do."

The Captain turned his attention to me, stone like and emotionless in his gaze. Before I could say anything, Vladislav had flipped the first switch, sending a jolt through me that took me off guard, and causing a scream to burst from me, more in surprise than pain. Vladislav smiled at this, and started tweaking his dial.

While his initial assault had been a surprise, we each soon discovered the true skill needed to actually win at this little game. The patterns were always changing, and a combination that hurt your opponent one moment caused a nauseating shock to you the next move. Or several moves would build in sequence, only to flash and spark and knock both players cold for a few moments. I couldn't tell if it was a game of moves and planning, or purely coincidence. But I couldn't stop now. Aside from the table in front of me, and the man who was trying to kill me, the rest of the room was all a shadow; everything except for Erin, who was still sleeping calmly next to Michaels. The distraction lifted my spirit, but cost me as Vladislav found a new combo and I found myself unable to move under my own strength, and my body convulsing uncontrollably. I could feel foam in my mouth, and a strange mixture of bile and blood on my lips. I threw up without warning, and hit the Captain dead in the face with a mixture of brown vomit, and almost florescent yellow bile. What didn't hit him landed on his controls, which momentarily shorted out, causing small leaps of lightening to hop across his hands.

Prospero called time, and switched the machine off long enough to clean off the panel.

"Kapitán! Vezmite si ju!" one of Vladislav's men cried.

"And exactly what is it you think I am *trying* to do?" The Captain replied, more snarky that I'd imagined he would ever sound.

It didn't take long before the machine was reset, and Prospero switched on the power. This time, I was the one to make the first move, flipping the first and forth switches, and turning the dial three quarters up in an instant. The resulting shock visibly took Vladislav by surprise, and he clamped his jaw shut with such force that he was soon spitting out broken teeth. I was soon returned the favor, and hit with a set of waves that caused my insides to feel as though they were seeing the light of day. I knew neither of us could take much more of this, not without permanent damage, or death. Now was the time to do anything necessary to win.

I thought back to my last time at this machine, when StrongArm had kicked me away from the table to break my hold and win the round. In that version of the game, only our feet were bound, this time, the game was more deadly, but only our hands were tied down to the metal plates. We couldn't let go if we wanted to, but as more and more jolts hit me, I had an idea that just might work.

"God love you, Granddaddy." I said aloud, thinking of him, my long gone Grandmother, and my mom. The three of them, along with my Aunt Chele had raised me, and had done so much to make sure I was well rounded in art, science, math, and overall living; Mom had insisted on the Martial Arts lessons, and I excelled in them. It was Aunt Chele who insisted on gymnastics, and after I learned to combine the two schools of study in my own unique way, I'd been banned from competition out of fairness to the other students.

I let the last wave subside, and stood up, my hands flat on the panel before me, fire red curls falling into my face.

"Vladislav!" I called out, my voice sounding dark and rough. He slowly brought his eyes up to me, reaching again for the dials and switches that he thought would seal my fate.

"What? Last words, child?"

"Only this." With that, I lifted my body with my arms, and arched my legs over backwards behind me, using them like claws to reach out over the table, and lift Vladislav up, then forced him onto the table across both sets of controls. The current that flew through me was almost unbearable, but I dare say that the inability to move probably helped me hold Vladislav down until the deed was done. The man's screams were cacophonic, echoing in the small space between our bodies. The smoke of burning flesh went right into my nose, making me reel and swoon. By the time the device shorted itself out, I collapsed to the table and ground. Landing on top of the old Smuggler, I could tell I'd won. He was not breathing, and his right eye had popped out of its socket. Blood leaked out of his skull, belying the fact that his heart was no longer forcing the life giving fluid through his veins.

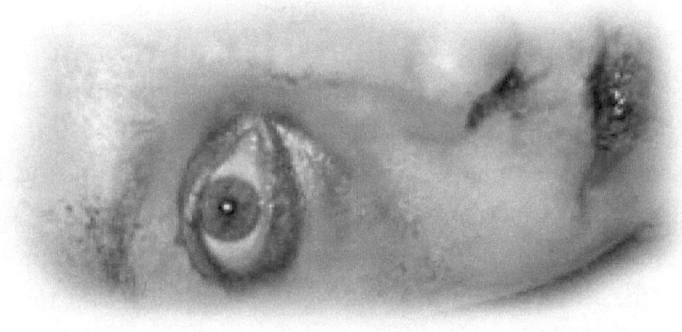

24
❧Selvage❧

"Well done, little girl." Prospero said, pushing the dead captain to the floor, his wrists still cuffed to the bidding machine. He unhooked my straps, and I suddenly discovered that my legs had turned to gelatin, and could no longer support me. I crumpled to the floor with a resounding thunk. Struggling to sit up, despite the tremors in my arms, stomach and legs, I was able to see the room again. Tiermo's men were still tied up in the corner. Vladislav's men were gone. Prospero noticed my looking about and filled in the blanks for me. "They fled after you killed their captain. Didn't even bother to untie their hands!"

I used what strength I could find to scoot my way over to Erin and Michaels. She was coming to, and more alert now than she'd been before my time spent bidding for her freedom.

"Ellie," She said softly. "Are you OK?

"I'm fine, love." I lied, reaching up with my right hand, barely able to direct it to cover hers. "We just need to get one thing, then we can go."

The sound of gunfire was once again tripping through the streets of the Zone. I'd actually been expecting it sooner. Before I had entered gate B3. I had used my new authority as Miami Director to notify the military of the threat to New Miami, and the possibility of bombs on the supports of the new city. From the sounds of it, troops had moved in, and had finally gotten close enough for us to hear the firefights.

"Oy!" I shouted to Prospero, with much less force than I'd hoped to muster. "A deal is a deal. Give me the trigger for Erin, and we'll be off."

Prospero reached into his coat pocket and pulled out a small triangular device with three flashing lights. "Keep it close to her." He tossed the device to me, knowing in my state that I couldn't possibly catch it. It fell to the floor, smashing into pieces. I didn't have the strength to fight anymore, and he knew it. The Bidding Machine had put me through all I could go through physically. Now, after all we'd done, I'd have to watch Erin die anyway.

Prospero laughed at the three of us, and reached over to the corner of the stage where Captain Vladislav had left the five million in gold.

"This works out well. For me, at least. I'll take this money, buy a new face, and start fresh. Maybe Boston would be a good choice." His guards called out to him, asking to take them with him, but he just chuckled and added, "Not to worry. Five million credits will buy me a lot of muscle in Boston!"

Prospero had evidently won, and he turned away from us all to leave the auction hall. One of his guards called out again, "Take us anyway! Besides, what if all the coins aren't there? You haven't even looked thru the sack yet!" This stopped Prospero in his tracks, and he quickly realized that he may have been had. He turned back toward the stage, and once it was reached, dumped the sack 's contents out for review. His men, and Tiermo's men, were now all offering their eternal loyalty, wiggling and writhing their way across the floor to surround Prospero as he inspected his Gold.

I looked up at Michaels. "Let's get out of here Aaron. We'll get Erin to a hospital and see what we can do for her."

Erin cocked her head and sleepily asked, "Why the hospital, Ellie?"

I didn't want to scare her, and as Michaels helped me to my feet, with my legs barely able to support my own weight, I answered, "Just to make sure you didn't get any stomach bugs while you were asleep in the Zone my love. That's all." Michaels picked Erin up in his right arm, and held the left for me to use as a crutch, and we hobbled toward the door. We only had a few steps left to take when I heard Prospero scream, "What is this!" I looked back, seeing Prospero turn the sack inside out to reveal what looked like a small electronic clock, plugged into a square of light brown material. Captain Vladislav had apparently also been an excellent chess player; planning his moves carefully and expecting the possibility of being double crossed, he'd planted a bomb in the middle of Prospero's treasure, and somehow, it had been triggered. We turned away and hobbled outside as fast as possible, looking back through the doorway only once we were at a safe distance. I saw Prospero struggling to move his massive weight through the men that had surrounded him. Stepping over them caused him to fall, and my last sight of Prospero Pizzano - the man who'd sold children, tortured me, and almost killed my girls, was of him trying to stand, only to be knocked down by the swarms of people around him, themselves each bound too tight to easily move away.

Then, the old Smuggler's bomb went off, bringing down the auction hall, and ridding the world of a monster and his henchmen.

25
❧Fallout❧

The Army units I had called in had broken protocol and landed in the Zone on two fronts, at the western gates, and at the waterfront. The armed militias that were made up of the Zone's inhabitants quickly found that having a gun and knowing *how* to use one were very different things, and they were either taken out, or rounded up as enemy combatants. When the Army forces reached our position outside the ruins of the Auction Hall, they ID'd us immediately, and called for ground transport to get us out. Michaels was on the verge of losing his eye, due to the pressure and swelling from his wounds. He told me later that Tiermo had knocked him to the ground, and used a cinder block to render him unconscious. Not only was his eye swollen almost to the point of no return, but his skull and cheekbones were either cracked or broken in six places.

As bad off as Michaels was, the Field medic that came to triage us found that I was in worse shape. With open wounds on my arms, electrical burns on random locations across my body, and a tremor that settled in my legs for a bit before hitting my entire body in waves, he said it was a miracle that my heart hadn't stopped or exploded. Even with all this, I knew I'd make it just fine. I was just worried about my girl.

After the trigger device had broken, it wasn't long before Erin started showing signs of fever, which spiked rapidly and uncontrollably. It took less than an hour to get the three of us out of the Zone, and out to St. Augustine's, but by the time we reached them, Erin was in and out of consciousness, with a fever reported at 106 degrees. I told the Doctors what I could between episodes of my body being racked with convulsions, and sure enough, when they looked at her blood, Carbon Nanotubes were present en masse. They immediately hooked Erin up to a filtering device, which was originally designed to cycle sickle cells out of the blood stream of African American children. With only a few tweaks, the device started filtering Erin's blood, and pulling out the Tubes that hadn't already released whatever poison they held.

****

Three days later, they released Michaels and me. Half of Aaron's head was in a printed cast, but part of his right eye was visible and open, even occasionally blinking a tiny bit. As for me, the Doctors had taken a sample of nerve cells from me, and used them to create a medication that would help stabilize the nerve damage I'd sustained, helping control the shakes and stopping the full body episodes outright. It would be a while before I'd be able to do many of the things I liked to do, but I was alive. My team and I had brought down one of the worst human traffickers in US History. We found out after ransacking the shipping company he'd run with Julian Sheldon, Prospero had been selling adults and children for almost a decade. But not anymore. We'd broken the crime family's hold over the Miami Zone. For the first time in fifteen years, Military boots were on the ground and in control there, and they were clearing out the people by the busload. Where they'd go was uncertain, but the Dark Zone in Miami was broken for good.

Discharged or not, I expected St. Augustine's to be my home until Erin recovered. The poisons

Prospero had placed in her body were actually not poisons at all; each chemical had been designed for medical use, and the Carbon Nanotubes had been designed to seek out a specific type of cancer that was rare in the United States. It was an experimental treatment because of the risks; the tubes were proven to target healthy neurons in people without the cancer. He had probably obtained the now illegal substance purely by a chance trade of flesh for profit. The doctors had worked hard on Erin, and had to bring her back at least twice. Now, she slept, IV's in each arm and leg, and a chest tube running down her side and to a collection bag.

If anyone had ever doubted that I would be a good parent - if *I* had ever doubted it myself, I realized, standing beside Erin's bed, looking at her like this, that I never had to worry about not being good enough, or trying to be perfect. As tough as it was to see her unconscious, fighting for her life with every breath, it was better than what would have happened. Some people give up on their children. To them, I have no words. I just don't understand, and I hope I never do.

The afternoon of my discharge, I called my mom to catch her up on things. As expected, Forrest had been keeping mom in the loop, but she was a bundle of nerves waiting to hear from me personally.

"How is my girl doing?" I asked as soon as mom had calmed down enough for me to get a word in edgewise.

"She is worried. She misses you." Mom paused, then added, "and *Chester* misses you too." It was now that, in the bottom of the frame of moms vidcall, I could see small hands sporadically moving in and out of frame.

"Mom, put the girl where I can see her!" I said. Mom quickly complied, and Olivia and Chester were soon looking at me over the view screen.

"Momma!" Olivia said, exasperation and surprise in her small voice. "What'n th' world did you *do* to yurself!" I know I looked rough, but I found myself giggling at Olivia, who was taking on the role of caregiver, and chiding me as best as she could for getting hurt.

"It looks worse than it is, my love." I answered, glad that she didn't have to see me go through what I had dealt with in the last few days. "As for what I did... well, I'd rather tell you in person."

"You're gonna be home soon?" She asked, making Chester's ears perk up as she talked.

"Not yet love. What I am doing is flying you and Nana to come see me. I have some things to tell you, and it just can't wait till I get home."

****

26
❧Reunion❧

"So what are you going to tell her, Ellie?" Mom asked. Olivia was asleep at her side on the flight from Mobile to Miami, and mom was taking the chance to see what I had planned.

I'd been pacing the floor of the Pedi-ICU waiting room. Visiting hours were limited, and since Erin wasn't in a private room, I couldn't camp out with her like I wanted to.

"I'm not sure, Mom. I've thought about it constantly for days." I sat back down, and looked at my mother's face on the handheld comm. "It would be different if I could just open a door, and they'd see each other. But that's out of the question."

Mom looked down to Olivia, and she moved her comm so I could see the little girl, sleeping soundly, with the edge of one of Chester's ears in her mouth.

"She hasn't had the nightmares lately, El." Mom offered. "Maybe a few twitches here and there, but not the waking in a puddle of sweat and urine that she went through a few months ago."

"I am so proud of her," was all I could say. Granddaddy used to say that folks that congratulated him on being such a good parent were missing the point. While he appreciated the sentiment, he always believed it was the kids who had the hardest job in growing up. I had come to the same conclusion long before I adopted.

"Let's just see how it goes, Mom." The sign announcing another window of visiting time lit up the waiting area, and I didn't want to miss a second. "I know I have to tell her something, and it might as well be the truth."

"But how much of the truth, Ellie?" Mom asked. I simply shrugged my shoulders, not knowing what the answer was. I blew my mother a kiss, and shut down the call. I'd figure out the answers soon enough, one way or the other.

****

Technically, I was still interim Director over the Miami District. I had passed along all those duties to Gallindo when I entered the Zone, and since I came out injured, hadn't bothered to take back any of the responsibility. I had only written one report, and I had dictated it while I was in the bathroom. Despite my lack of Managerial Duties, and the small fact that I had no intention of staying in Miami a second longer than I had to, I still called in a favor, and had Gallindo pick Mom and Olivia up from the Airport, and deliver them to St. Augustine's.

I knew my Mom wanted to see me, hug me, and nearly kill me with affection, so I was surprised and proud when she let Olivia run to me in the waiting area, and held herself back to let me have my own mother-daughter moment. Olivia started crying as she jumped into my arms and held on tight, but they were tears of joy, and not the tears of fear she'd cried too many times in her short life.

"Momma!" She cried, not able to find the words for feelings she couldn't even describe. I held her close, and took her head in my hand, gently caressing the back of her noggin and kissing her temples and cheeks.

"Livy, my love!" I held her up so I could see her. "I am so glad to see you! I think you've grown six inches since I saw you last!"

Through her tears, Olivia giggled. "That's what Chester told me you'd say! We've been eating a lot of cereal!"

I hugged Olivia close again, then sat back on the sofa I'd claimed as my own.

"What happened, Momma?" Olivia asked again, only this time, I could tell she wasn't going to wait long for an answer.

I proceeded to tell my girl things I hadn't told her before. Things about losing Erin that I thought would only hurt her, I could now tell her because there was a different ending. I told her how Erin had gotten away from the explosion, but was held by one of the bad men who'd hurt them before. I glazed over what it took to get in and find her sister, and hardly even mentioned the bidding machine, or what it had done to me in my effort to get her sister. I think half of everything I said after 'Erin is alive' didn't even go in one ear and out the other side; I think it bypassed her noggin completely, falling into the background of her excitement.

When I told her Erin had gotten hurt on the way out, her happiness immediately abated. She was suddenly very serious.

"I wanna see Erin, Momma." She stated bluntly. "I wanna see my sister."

I stood as best as I could, feeling the medication wearing thin in my bloodstream and catching a few quivers as they passed through my legs, and took Olivia's hand. Normally, children weren't allowed in Pedi-ICU as visitors, but I had pulled a few strings (and Zim had hacked into the hospital computer to help) and made sure that getting Livy into see her sister wouldn't be a problem.

Olivia clung to my side as we walked through the darkened, almost silent ward. Aside from the flicker of lights from medical equipment, and the soft sounds of breathing machines and monitors, the room was oppressively quite. When we reached Erin's bed, I pulled out a small stool, and sat her on top so she could get a good look at her sister.

Erin was sleeping peacefully, and the nurses had removed a few of the IV's. Still, she hadn't woken since we arrived at the hospital, and while the poisons and Nanotubes were out of her little body, there was no way to tell when, or even if, she'd wake up.

Olivia stood up on the stool, and climbed into the hospital bed with her sister, putting her small arms around her twin, just like they had when I first met them. A few tears escaped Olivia's eyes, but she held them back, whispering to her sister, "You gotta come home, Erin. I gotta take care of you and Momma."

I leaned over the girls, and kissed them both on the forehead just like I had for every night we'd been together, and placed Chester between Olivia and Erin. Maybe it was the touch of her sister, or maybe it was the odd, slightly musty smell of the old rabbit that started to hit home, but after a moment or two, Erin moved her hand up to hold Chester, then reached out to her sister with her other hand. Olivia was almost asleep already, but noticed her sister's touch instantly.

"See, Momma? " Livy said as she drifted off. "Chester said it would all be ok."

27
❧Christmas❧

It never snowed in Mobile. When my Granddad was young, he told us that our 'City of Six Flags' would occasionally get some snow. Aside from a quarter inch of frost that many southerners called 'snow', I hadn't seen so much as a flake since my training months in Northern New England.

This being our first Christmas together, I made sure I went all out. It may have been eighty degrees outside, but in my Victorian-Styled apartment home on the one hundred twenty fifth floor, you would never know it. I turned the thermostat down as low as it would go, and got a can of spray frost and snow from the hobby store, taking time over the past few days to gingerly decorate every window. We had a fire going in the fireplace, food and snacks by the pound, and enough hot chocolate for everyone.

We went all out on the decorations too. Mom had been staying with us since Erin came home from the hospital, and the girls' time in the Miami Zone was starting to become a distant dream, only recalled when necessary. I had figured that neither of my girls had ever had a proper Christmas, and together with my mother and my aunt Chele, we pulled out all the stops. The tree was live, and twelve feet tall. Garland and tinsel wound their way to the top of the fir giant, gently caressing glass balls of all sizes and colours. English Crackers sat in the branches, eagerly waiting to play their role in the festivities, and more than a few presents were tucked away in the delicate branches here and there. The lights were the **coup de grâce**, changing colours often and doing every dance from a slow fade to a gentle twinkle.

On Christmas Eve, the girls sat in my arms by the fire, with the soft glow of the tree illuminating an old copy of 'T'was the Night Before Christmas'. I read the story to them, adding sounds effects and accents to make the tale come alive, just as my mother, grandfather and his father had for generations before. The traditional milk and cookies were laid out for Santa, and even a few carrot sticks were left for his reindeer. By the time their little heads hit the pillow, each girl was completely worn out. As I tucked them in, Erin opened her eyes slightly, and held up Chester to me.

"He didn't get a goodnight kiss, Momma." Erin said, barely able to keep her eyes open.

"He most certainly did, young lady!" I exclaimed, leaning over to kiss the old rabbit again. "But I don't think one more will hurt anything."

Erin pulled Chester back, and placed him in between herself and Olivia. They still shared a bed, but considering all my girls had been through, I didn't care how long they slept at each other's side.

"Night, Momma."

I turned to leave the girl's room, and stopped at the door to switch off the light.

"Good night, my loves." I said quietly, carefully pulling the old oak door closed.

****

Christmas morning was a flurry of excited children, a tired grandmother, and me taking pictures of every moment. The girls had come downstairs just at sunrise, sleepily rubbing the sand from their eyes and dragging Chester between them. The sight of all the presents under the tree immediately brought them up to full speed, and Olivia and Erin each bounced the rest of the way into the living room. We had music playing, a holiday parade showing on the viewer, and breakfast already set up at the table - buffet style - so we could come and go from the table as we wished.

I had tried to keep a lid on the amount of presents we got for the girls. I didn't want them to be overwhelmed with 'things'. Of course, *Nana Clause* snuck in a few extra presents for each, and before I knew it, they both had a small hoard of toy unicorns and ponies, dragons and pirates, makeup, costumes, and pretty much anything else an almost five year old little girl might want for her fantasies. Even Chester racked up, getting a new coat to go with the pants Olivia had insisted we buy him for Thanksgiving (she'd been convinced that he couldn't come to the table naked on a holiday). We were just getting ready to start clearing up the wrapping paper when my door chime rang. I looked at Mom, and she looked at me, shrugging.

"Aunt Chele flew out yesterday to be with Ren, didn't she?" I asked, knowing full well my darling aunt had gone to spend the holiday with her daughter in California.

I tied my robe together as I walked to the door, but nothing could have prepared me for who I saw when I opened it.

"Granddaddy!" It was the first time I'd seen my Grandfather out of a hospital bed in years. There he stood, with his black fedora covering his silver and white hair, wire frame spectacles, neatly trimmed goatee, and wearing his best ruby red brocade vest, coat and pocket watch. I almost leapt on the old man in excitement. "What are you doing out of the Hospital?!"

My grandfather returned the tight embrace, then pulled back enough to look me in the eyes.

"I was tired of being there, Ellie, and I needed to get out. Needed to get out before there was nothing left of me. Figured that this was probably the best place I could go on Christmas Morning." He then muttered something about trying to get cab a on Christmas morning being damned near impossible. It was now that I noticed he had two pieces of luggage propped up next to my door.

Granddad looked to the ground when I noticed his bags, and his already quiet voice went down another level. "Um, Ellie? I was thinking..."

My grandfather was not an arrogant man, but he did have his pride. I had learned many years ago that it was hard for him to accept help, or even ask for help.

Granddaddy continued, "I wasn't getting any worse, but the Hospital was draining the life out of me. I figured that I could either spend my time dying, or take what I have and spent it living. I don't know if I have five years, or five minutes of breath in me, but I'd like it to be spent with you and the girls, if I can."

"I don't know, Granddaddy," I said, reaching out into the hall and grabbing his bags, placing them just inside my foyer. "Two little girls can be an awful lot of work for an old fella like you." I winked as I said this, stepping aside to welcome him in.

"Don't I know it!" he replied, closing the door behind him. "Well, it'll all work out for the best, then. Doctors tell me I should have dementia in a few years. You think you have your hands full now, you just wait till you have to go and catch me running around the apartment complex in nothing but my birthday suit and a smile!"

I took Granddaddy's hand in mine, and we walked together into the living room, surprising Mom and confusing the girls. Granddaddy walked over to them, and they each stood close, to get a good look at him.

"Where's your red suit, Santa?" Erin asked my grandfather, tugging gently at his sleeve.

"Shouldn't you be resting, Sir?" Olivia asked him. "You were up *all night*!"

My mom stood up and hugged her father, then knelt down beside Erin. "Honey, this isn't Santa Clause; it's my father."

"Your *Great* Grandfather." I added, kneeling next to Olivia. "He's coming to live with us."

Mom's shock was evident, but happy tears quickly filled her eyes. "Daddy?" She asked, "Are you sure?"

"Why not, my loves!" my Grandfather answered. "I raised you, and Ellie; and I still have some time ahead of me. Maybe not as much as I have behind me, but I can still help. Besides," he paused, dropping to the floor and sitting crossed legged in front of the girls, taking them each gently and putting one on each knee, "where else will you find a free babysitter?"

We all settled in on the floor in the living room, surrounded by the sights and smells of Christmas, with little ones playing in our laps. While I wished my friends could have been here with us, I knew that now, with Erin and Olivia safely home, and my mother and grandfather at my side, my family was more complete than it had even been.

⮧Epilogue⮦

Galeno Tiermo stood on the old wooden dock, smoking a cigarette and looking out into the night at the cold, black water. Piracy was proving to be a much harder way of life than he'd imagined when he'd made his deal to get out of the Zone in Miami. With their Captain dead, what few members of the crew that escaped took the opportunity to get back to their sub, and they took Tiermo with them. Now, as he pulled a threadbare coat closer to his body in hopes of trapping some of his warmth from escaping into the cold Norwegian air, Tiermo was thinking of revenge.

The turret of the *MURDERER'S SLAVE* crested the water close to the pier, allowing Tiermo to step carefully from land to sea, and enter his new home. Passing along shipping info he'd stolen from a warehouse office in Oslo, Tiermo removed his coat, and made his way to the galley. Food was scarce on board, but he'd managed to bring in a few loaves of bread and snacks hidden under his clothes. Now, as it was with everything else on board, the food he'd recovered belonged to all of them.

Weeks had passed since Tiermo had been abroad, and each night he spent on the ship, he performed the same ritual. He'd sit in his cabin, light a red candle, and focus himself, not in calm meditation, but in hateful contemplation. He'd snagged a picture of Ellyandra from one of the Miami news sites, and took the archaic step of actually printing dozens of copies. In his mind, she'd ruined his easy life, and tossed him out of a world of privilege into the horror of privateering. Each night, after working himself into an exhausted rage from stabbing and hitting the image over and over, he finally crumpled the paper, and tossed the image of his hated opponent into the candle flame, watching eagerly as the paper blacked with an extension of his anger and contempt.

The sea churned around the *MURDERER'S SLAVE*; Tiermo slept, dreaming dreams of revenge as the ship made its way around the globe, heading slowly - eventually - back to his target.

❧finis❧

If you don't want any spoilers, don't read any further!

If, however, you are interested, turn the page for the prologue of MURDER: BOOK THREE.

Watch www.derekdykes.com for release information!

MURDER: BOOK THREE

❧prologue❧

Oppressive was not a strong enough word to describe the summertime heat in Mobile. Being located in lower Alabama, right on the Gulf of Mexico, the humidity only added additional levels of discomfort. Of course, my mother had loved growing up here; she was always cold, no matter how hot it was. I, on the other hand, had an unnaturally high body temp, and like my grandfather, could never seem to get comfortable when the ambient temperature was over seventy-five. I found myself looking across the square and over the old buildings of Mobile's Historic District at the hazy silhouette of New Mobile, almost wishing that my next case was in the Dark Zone that existed in its shadow, just so I could cool off.

The three tiered fountain in Bienville Square offered its cooling mist to me as I entered the center of the park. Despite the already high humidity, the water coming off the fountain always seemed cool, and made it tolerable to be outside. I could see my team, along with several policemen, surrounding one of the decades-old wrought iron benches that circled the fountain, each one backing up to a flower bed and bushes of various types. When I got close enough, I could see bare feet sticking out of the foliage.

Zimmerman stood, staring at the body, hands in his pockets and a blank look in his eyes. Zim had a tough time dealing with the dead, especially after St. Louis, when his fiancée had been violently killed in the Dark Zone. He was holding his own, and doing a lot better, but Zim still had his moments when he retreated into the safety of his mind. I knew he'd be there when I needed him. More importantly, I'd be there when he needed me.

Michaels was tapping away at the control unit for a MR-CSA (Mobile Robotic Crime Scene Analyzer) that he'd brought to the scene. He looked up long enough to acknowledge me, and turned immediately back to monitoring the MR-CSA as it continued its E-MRI scan of the body.

"What do we have today, boys?" I asked sleepily. The coffee had not yet hit my brain and it had been a very long week.

"Well Ellie, this is what we in the forensics lab of the FBI refer to as a corpse. Although from the identification in the victim's wallet, we could call him Mr. Preston Woodridge."

I gave Michaels a look and reached out to take the ID. The holographic photo of Mr. Woodridge matched the face of the man lying on the ground. His right cheek was pressed into the dirt and there were bloodless scratches on his visible cheek, likely caused by the branches he'd fallen into.

"No blood in the facial abrasions; he was dumped here". I said, bringing out a small penlight to illuminate the victim's remains. "His skin looks glossy, Aaron. Any idea what the substance is?"

Michaels checked the MR-CSA controls, and shuffled through the data on the small, handheld screen. "Nope - the scan is finishing up now, but the data hasn't all been processed".

"Did he have any family, Ellie?" Zim asked quietly. He'd been like this for a week; even though he had made great strides since the incident, this was a back step, and I wasn't sure why it was happening. I stood up and took my own handheld out of my pocket, and accessed the main database using the deceased' National ID number.

"Looks like he has a sister here in Mobile, and a brother in Queens," I answered, feeling a knot suddenly grow in my stomach. I hated having to give people news like this.

My attention turned back to the crime scene and I continued to examine the body. His clothes were almost new; the pants still had threads on the back pocket where the paper label had been attached. A mass of black curly hair covered his head, but he was well groomed and clean cut from all I could see. I gloved my hand and reached out to lift the victims arm, but found it was completely immobile.

"Wow. Rigor has already set in." I turned my attention to one of the policemen keeping people away from the scene. "Who's in charge of your unit, Officer?"

The young officer pointed to an older man who was standing fifteen feet away. I whistled to get his attention, then smiled and motioned for him to come toward me.

"When was the last patrol before the body was discovered?" I asked.

"Three AM. We send out regular patrols every three hours since the zone opens up into the historic district only two blocks away."

"So the body was discovered at six, then?" I asked, mapping a timeline in my head.

"Yes Ma'am. Officer McDonald was coming through to do his rounds as a litter crew was doing their weekly on the foliage. They converged on this area just as Officer McDonald did, and he called it in immediately."

Our conversation was cut short when the MR-CSA scanning the scene sounded a warning siren. Red lights started flashing on its dome, continuing to do so even after Michaels cut the siren so we could all hear.

"Hazard Warning Ellie!", Michaels called. "The E-MRI has picked up an unknown biohazard. Whatever it is, it's been tagged as lethal."

The squad of police officers each took several steps back, leaving me and my boys up close and personal with the apparently tainted corpse.

"Damnit!" I shouted, reaching into the MR-CSA and pulling out a large glass vial with a cutting tool built into the top. I took the device and used it to envelop the deceased' forefinger. With a sharp turn of the metal iris atop the lid, the finger was quickly and cleanly removed. It dropped into the built-in hazard container that sealed itself immediately.

"Got a sample; lock it down, Michaels" I said, quickly backing away with Zimmerman. Michaels backed away too, all the while tapping in new commands into the Mobile Analyzer. The MR-CSA extended one of its few appendages, which flipped over and opened, revealing a laser which it aimed at the body. Usually we used recovery drones to burn away the dead that tended to pile up in the dark zone, but MR-CSA's were equipped with hazard removal lasers as well, for situations just like this. The laser beam fired, but instead of beginning the process of destroying the almost ceramic-looking tissue, the beam refracted from the corpse as soon as it had burned through the clothes, and hit a nearby storefront, knocking bricks and mortar onto the ground below. Michaels hit a different control, and the colour of the beam shifted from red to blue, and widened two-fold. The more powerful laser beam stopped refracting, and within seconds all that was left of the remains was a large, black smudge on the ground.

Smoke wafted up from the place where the body of Mr. Woodridge had lain only moments before, and the police officers all gathered close to look at the carnage. Zim and Michaels gathered close to me as I held up the only remaining portion of the deceased. In the small jar, closed tight for safety, sat a whitish, almost porcelain-looking finger. When I shook the jar, the finger tinkled against the glass, sounding like a piece of pottery being shaken in a vial.

****

www.ingramcontent.com/pod-product-compliance
Lightning Source LLC
Chambersburg PA
CBHW020725210626
46807CB00016B/115